The suspect noticed the pair of them sitting surveillance in the car

"He's trying to get a look at us," Keegan whispered. He turned and India couldn't figure out what he was up to until he reached for her. "Sorry," he mumbled as he cupped her face with his big hands and lowered his mouth over hers.

She fought him but he was strong; she could barely move, barely breathe…but she could feel.

Where their mouths met, she felt a hot sizzle of electricity. It crackled through her body, igniting her from within. She saw the bright, shifting images that played through his mind…her eyes, her lips…the suspect looking back over his shoulder.…

Such warm lips…I knew they'd feel like this.… Was that her or Keegan? She felt exasperated and frustrated and aroused, all at once, and she had no idea whose feelings were whose.

Patricia Ryan is the winner of the 1994 Golden Heart Award for Best Short Contemporary Romance. The book, *The Return of the Black Sheep*, was published by Harlequin Temptation. Pat grew up on Long Island and wrote fiction from early childhood, as did her twin sister. She studied art and writing and earned a Bachelor of Fine Arts in painting—a degree that ensures its recipient of absolute unemployability. After a stint as a paralegal and with a publisher promoting other people's books, Pat started to write for real. And she's been quite a success! Pat is also the author of two historical romances. Her twin sister, in case you were wondering, is being published by Harlequin Intrigue.

Books by Patricia Ryan

HARLEQUIN TEMPTATION
540—THE RETURN OF THE BLACK SHEEP

A BURNING TOUCH
Patricia Ryan

Harlequin Books

TORONTO • NEW YORK • LONDON
AMSTERDAM • PARIS • SYDNEY • HAMBURG
STOCKHOLM • ATHENS • TOKYO • MILAN
MADRID • WARSAW • BUDAPEST • AUCKLAND

To my mother,
Sue Smith Burford

ISBN 0-373-25671-X

A BURNING TOUCH

Copyright © 1996 by Patricia Burford Ryan.

Printed in U.S.A.

Prologue

"WHAT DO YOU think you're doing?"

India eyed her husband warily as she unbuckled her sandals by the back door. "Just going for a walk."

Perry closed his eyes. That vein on his forehead started pulsing.

He had never understood why she liked to go off all by herself for these long walks along the shore. And on this particular late August afternoon, not only were storm clouds gathering over Cape Cod Bay, but there was company to entertain. His mother and sisters had just arrived for one last visit before he closed up the summerhouse for the season.

"All I want," he said between clenched teeth, "is for you to play the role of the gracious hostess for three, maybe four, hours. You're my wife. Do you think you can manage to stick around and act the part for just one damn afternoon?" He raked his manicured fingers through his prematurely gray hair, then smoothed it back in place.

When she'd married Perry—had it really been just ten months ago?—that steel-colored hair had been one of the things she'd found most attractive about him. He'd reminded her of Richard Gere in *Pretty Woman*. She'd never in her life known any man as sophisticated and worldly, and she couldn't believe her good fortune when, after a dazzling six-week courtship, he'd asked her to be his wife.

But recently, between the hair and that tight-lipped, censorious scowl of his, he was reminding her more and more of her father. When he launched into one of his increasingly frequent lectures on her image and behavior, the resemblance became downright eerie. Last night, as she lay in bed, she'd found herself imagining what it would feel like to pack her things, get in her little Saab, and drive away. All by herself. It had been a remarkably satisfying fantasy.

"I'll be back in half an hour," she said carefully as she kicked off the sandals and squatted down to roll up the legs of her jeans. "Please, Perry. I'll play whatever role and act whatever part you want when I get back. But right now I need thirty minutes for myself, and then I can—"

"No!" He yanked her roughly to her feet and shook her. "Right now you need to serve some drinks to Mother and Kitty and Gracie. They'll never change their opinion of you if you don't stop running off whenever they—"

"They'll never change their opinion of me, period." She twisted out of his grip and rubbed her arms. His rough handling of her was a recent unnerving development, causing her to wonder whether that ultracivilized facade of his was just that—a facade. "They act like I'm something they want to swat away."

"If you'd only try—"

"I'm not one of them." She lifted her chin, but her quavering voice betrayed her frustration, her growing sense of futility. "You didn't marry a debutante from Newport, Perry. You married a middle-class lawyer's daughter from humble Mansfield, New Jersey. I'm not a socialite, I'm a veterinarian, a working woman. I have a career and goals and interests that have nothing to do with the polo circuit or cotillions. Your mother and Kitty and Gracie are just going to have to learn to accept that."

Turning toward the beach, she took a deep breath and added, "And so are you."

MAYBE I SHOULD head back, India thought, inspecting the sky. It was menacingly gray over the water, but still blue overhead. She turned and looked back toward the house. Even at this distance, she could make out Perry, all in white, and the three willowy blondes, in pastel linen sheaths, leaning on the railing of the upstairs deck. The late afternoon sun polished their bronzed limbs and glinted off their silvery martinis. A ripple of female laughter wafted toward her on the salty breeze.

She sighed. *Just ten more minutes, then I'll go back.* She checked her watch and continued walking, reveling in the precious solitude, a solitude she had coveted since childhood. Only when she was alone was there no role to play, no image to project. She gave herself over to the caress of warm sand beneath her bare feet, the reassuring cadence of waves slapping the shore.

Ten minutes later, she decided, *I'll go back when it starts to rain.* A soft rumble rolled through the air, but the sun still shone. She had time before the storm hit.

When she reached the public beach, it was deserted. The parking lot, off to her right past the dunes, was empty. A sudden discharge of thunder crashed all around her, and she jumped.

All right, all right, I give up. With a grudging acceptance of the inevitable, she turned and took a step toward home.

INDIA OPENED HER EYES.

She lay on her back, rain pelting her. Beneath her she felt, not sand, but hard concrete pavement. Panic raced through her when she tried to move her arms, then her legs, and couldn't. She could barely breathe, and her heart hammered crazily in her chest. The rain skewered her with pain.

A thunderclap detonated overhead, followed by dazzling rivulets that crackled across the darkened sky.

I've been hit by lightning, she thought with amazement. Inch by inch, she lifted her head. Looking around, she saw that she'd been thrown a good twenty yards, from the beach into the parking lot. When she lowered her head, pain clamored inside her skull.

Some time passed before she was able to heave herself into a sitting position. Looking down, she saw blood, lots of it, on herself and the pavement. Everything hurt. She knew she'd cracked one or two ribs, and maybe her collarbone. When she could lift her right hand, she gently touched her face, and winced. The left side felt swollen and sticky.

The closest house was a cedar-shingled rental cottage a couple of hundred feet away. A red station wagon sat in front, and there were lights on in the windows. She tried to stand, but the soles of her feet were charred, and the pain was excruciating. So she crawled with agonizing slowness in the rain, over concrete and then sand, until finally—after what seemed an eternity—she reached the front door of the cottage. She collapsed against it and tried to knock, but neither hand would form a fist. Her attempt to cry out was useless, too; she had no control over her throat.

Again and again she shoved her shoulder against the door, until finally it opened, and she tumbled onto a braided rug.

"Oh, my God!" a woman's voice cried as India slipped into unconsciousness. "Frank! Call 911!"

SHE CAME TO, and realized she was moving. Luminous fluorescent tubes streaked by overhead and she watched them with a kind of hypnotic detachment. A muffled rumbling surrounded her, and the air smelled coldly antiseptic. She surmised that she lay on a gurney being wheeled through the corridor of a hospital, and felt a sense of overwhelming relief.

They'll take care of me here. I'll be okay.

She lapsed in and out of consciousness several times over the next few hours, dimly aware of them giving her an EKG and a lot of X rays. They injected her with painkillers and antibiotics, cleaned her wounds, treated what they called exit burns on the soles of her feet, and set her collarbone. She had left home without any ID, so they kept asking her for her name, but her mouth wouldn't form the words properly, and they couldn't make sense of the sounds that came out of her. They gave her a pencil with which to write, but her fingers refused to close around it.

Even in her near insensible haze, she became increasingly aware of something odd happening whenever someone touched her. A flickering image, like a TV picture with bad reception, would hover in her mind's eye and then dissolve before she could make sense of it. A bewildering array of feelings accompanied the images. What troubled her most was that something about this phenomenon was strikingly familiar to her, but she couldn't quite place why. Weary and confused, she decided the electrical signals in her brain had gone haywire when the lightning zapped her, and she hoped the effect was temporary.

Finally they wheeled her into a room and left her alone. She fell asleep, only to be awakened during the night by one of the nurses, a middle-aged woman with hair like a shiny yellow helmet.

"Are you India Cook Milbank?"

India nodded. "Y-yes." She grinned, delighted as much by her ability to voice a word as by the fact that they knew who she was.

The nurse nodded to someone in the hall, who entered the room—Perry. For the first time in a long time, she was actually glad to see him, but when he got a good look at her, his eyes grew wide and his mouth fell open. Well, what could she expect? She knew what she must look like. Despite their recent difficulties, his was a comfortingly familiar face. She found herself reaching out to him, and he hesitantly took her hand.

The TV in her mind instantly clicked on. She saw her own face, in jittery patterns of light and dark, gazing into the "camera"—into Perry's eyes. She saw the discolored swelling, the lacerations on her cheeks and forehead, the singed black hair in tangled disarray, and knew without a doubt that this was exactly what Perry viewed.

Not again. Suddenly she understood, with horrible clarity, what was so familiar about this ability to conjure up ghostlike pictures in her mind, pictures of other people's thoughts. She had had this ability before, a long time ago, and it had nearly ruined her life. Now the lightning had reawakened it.

To see herself through Perry's eyes was bad enough, but there was more. A wave of disgust swelled within her, pure and powerful and uncomplicated by feelings of love

or tenderness or affection of any kind. What she felt—
or rather, what Perry felt and transmitted to her by his
touch—was simple repugnance. He viewed her not as a
loved one to be comforted, but as a thing to be dealt with.
An irritating thing. An ugly thing. A disgusting thing.

"India! You're hurting me! Let go!" Her grip had tightened involuntarily. She tried to loosen her fingers, but
they wouldn't budge. He tried to shake her off. "Let go,
damn it!"

The nurse managed to pry her fingers open. "There,
now. Isn't it nice to have your husband here? I can make
up a cot if you'd like, and he can stay the night. Wouldn't
that be—"

"G-get him out," India gasped, her voice a thick slur.
Perry and the nurse exchanged a look, but she didn't
care. "L-leave me alone, Perry."

"Now, dear." The nurse rested a hand on her arm, and
India saw her own face, wild-eyed and terrified, and
knew what the nurse was thinking . . . *A good strong
sedative . . .*

"N-no!" She swatted clumsily at the nurse, wincing at
the pain that coursed through her. "G-go away! Don't
touch me!"

Perry closed a hand over her shoulder. She saw herself again, felt his revulsion again. "India, stop this.
Now!" He turned to the nurse. "Can't you give her
something?"

"Don't touch me!" India screamed, writhing and flail-
ing at him. "Don't touch me, don't touch me! Leave me
alone!" Other people came into the room. Strong hands
held her down while she struggled, her mind a kaleido-
scope of disjointed images and sensations. Someone

gripped her arm painfully. She felt an icy scrub of alcohol, followed by the sting of a needle.

"Leave me alone," she moaned as her muscles relaxed and her eyelids grew heavy. "I just want to be alone. That's all I ever wanted."

1

DETECTIVE LIEUTENANT James Keegan bounded up the back steps of the Mansfield, New Jersey, police station, threw open the door, and sang out, "Honey, I'm home!"

The desk sergeant, leathery Al Albonetti, glanced up from his paperwork without moving his head or altering his perpetually bored expression. "Morning, Lieutenant. Captain wants to see you, some lady's waiting for you in your office, and, uh . . ." His gaze slid toward an elderly woman scowling in the corner.

"It's about time, Keegan," she growled as she pulled a steno pad from the pocket of her parka and flipped it open. Sylvia Hazelett was a wizened little bird of a woman, but she had the voice of a three-pack-a-day teamster.

The detective unbuttoned his trench coat with one hand and held the other palm out as he backed away. "Sorry, Sylvie, but I'm late this morning as it is, and—"

"A five-minute interview, Jamie." She slipped on the reading glasses that hung around her neck. "I go to press tomorrow, and the *Courier*'s just a weekly, so if I wait to get this story, it'll be dead news by the time my readers see it."

"What story?"

Sergeant Albonetti sighed. "That's what Captain Garrett wants to brief you on, Lieutenant."

"The arson story," Sylvie said.

He groaned. "Don't tell me—"

"Another note came this morning," the sergeant said. "Signed 'The Firefly,' same as the other three. Says he's gonna do it again sometime this week."

Jamie spat out a ripe obscenity. The first note had come three weeks ago, the eleventh of October to be exact. Four days later, in the middle of the night, the contents of the Dumpster behind the Stop 'n Save went up in flames. Everyone had been relieved that it wasn't worse. A few days later, there'd been another note, followed by another, somewhat more destructive, fire. The framework of a house under construction in an upscale subdivision had been torched. People started to get nervous. The third note had precipitated a flurry of anxious speculation as to the Firefly's next target. It turned out to be Little Eddie's, a roadhouse on the edge of town. The single-story clapboard structure had swiftly burned to the ground in the wee hours of the morning, a week ago. Thankfully, the arsonist had waited until after closing time to set the blaze. So far, his attacks had claimed no human victims, and Jamie wanted to end them before that changed.

Sylvie clicked her pen. "Each fire's been a little more ambitious than the last. Do you expect that trend to continue?"

"What do *you* think?" Jamie asked.

She peered at him over her reading glasses. "I think you better catch this guy before he barbecues the whole town."

"That's excellent advice, Sylvie. Now, if you'll excuse me—"

She grabbed his arm. "Everyone in town knows you're in charge of the arson investigation. You've been pulled off everything else, right?" Jamie nodded. "Then I can't help but wonder if the woman who's waiting for you upstairs has something to do with the case. Maybe she knows something about the note that came today."

With a sigh, Jamie turned to Sergeant Albonetti. "Does she?"

"Dunno, Lieutenant. All's I know is, she showed up at the front desk about forty-five minutes ago, asking for you."

"I saw her," Sylvie interjected. "Quite the hot ticket—for Mansfield, anyway. Black hair, shades. Looked vaguely familiar, but I couldn't quite place her. What do you think—is she here about the arson case?"

Jamie shrugged. "I guess there's a better than even chance. If you want to wait around till after I talk to her—"

"I don't 'wait around,' Keegan. Life's too short." She tucked her notebook away and took off her glasses, a mischievous spark in her eyes. "She's probably just one of your conquests, anyway."

He cocked an eyebrow. "One of my conquests? You overestimate my appeal, Sylvie."

"Honey, you're tall, dark and handsome. Not to mention employed. That's a winning formula all by itself, but throw in that nice Irish brogue—"

"I don't have a brogue."

"You do, just a residual one. I mean, it doesn't sound like you just got off the boat. You came here, what—a good ten or fifteen years ago, right?"

"Twenty-five."

"Oh. Well, it's very slight. It comes out mostly when you're all worked up over something. That's what really puts you over the top. I guarantee you there are a dozen women in Mansfield alone who'd sell their souls to be able to pour your Cheerios in the morning."

"If you run into one, would you get me her number? It's been a while since I've had my Cheerios poured."

Her eyebrows shot up. "Hard to believe."

He grinned. "I'm saving it for you, Sylvie, but you persist in playing hard to get."

"I wondered why you were always undressing me with your eyes."

"Lieutenant." Sergeant Albonetti cocked his head toward a lanky, shirtsleeve figure leaning against the doorframe of the roll call room.

Jamie nodded. "Captain. You wanted to see me?"

"Take your time, Lieutenant." Twenty years in Mansfield, New Jersey, hadn't made much of an inroad in Sam Garrett's lazy Texas drawl. With his weather-beaten face and thick shock of salt-and-pepper hair, he looked every inch the displaced, aging cowboy. Glancing from Jamie to Sylvie, he said, "I can wait till you've finished attempting to seduce Ms. Hazelett."

Sylvie zipped up her parka. "If I weren't twice his age, I'd give him a run for his money." She strode purposefully out the door.

Garrett's expression sobered. He held up a sheet of paper. Jamie walked over and took it from him. It was a photocopy of a note that had been spelled out, like the last one, with letters snipped from magazines: "My matchbook is whispering to me. Something burns this week. The Firefly."

Garrett said, "The original's at the lab with the documents examiner, but I can tell you right now, he's not gonna find a damn thing we can use. There won't be any prints, of course."

"Not unless he suddenly decides to slip up. So, what have we got?"

"We got us a pyro who means to torch another building in Mansfield sometime between tonight and next Monday. If he sticks to his favorite M.O., he'll strike in the early morning hours and use kerosene as an accelerant. Am I missing anything? It's your case."

"He probably uses matches, rather than a cigarette or a candle or some other igniter that would delay the flames till he's had a chance to get away."

"How do you know?"

"He just told us so, in his note."

The captain grunted. "Smart-ass."

"But other than that—" he shrugged "—I don't have a clue. No useful evidence, no motive.... Where the hell do I start?"

"Why don't you start with that visitor I hear you've got waiting for you upstairs? Find out what she wants. If there's any connection whatsoever to this case, I suggest you get to the bottom of it, pronto."

Jamie folded up the photocopy and stuck it in a pocket of his coat. "You got it."

Upstairs, he poured two foam cups full of coffee, then stood outside the glass door of his tiny office, studying the woman seated on the little metal chair in front of his desk. When his aunt Bridey had taught him how to do this, she'd called it "sizing up the mark." Years later, when Professor Mayhew had taught him the same skills for use in criminal investigation, *he'd* called it "visual preanalysis of the interviewee." Whatever you called it, it amounted to the same thing, a cataloging of the subject's features and actions in order to pinpoint various characteristics. In Aunt Bridey's case, the characteristics she looked for were wealth and gullibility. Professor Mayhew had expanded this list to include trustworthiness, cooperativeness, secretiveness—anything that might help or hinder the police detective in his work.

By Jamie's estimation, the woman waiting for him was thirty to thirty-five years of age. She had chin-length black hair, pale skin, a slender frame, and looked to be of medium height. She wore faded blue jeans, but that was the only color on her body. Her turtleneck, boots and shoulder bag were black, as were the Ray•Ban sunglasses that hid her eyes from view and the dyed shearling coat hung on the corner rack. She even had on black leather gloves, although it was just early November, and a mild day at that.

Also, she'd been indoors for almost an hour, so why the gloves? Or the sunglasses? People communicated with their hands and eyes. To cover them up like that was an unmistakable signal: *Leave me alone.*

The signal was echoed in her posture—legs tightly crossed, arms wrapped around her torso. Ditto the all-black attire, as if a spot of color might draw too much attention to her. But if she wanted to be left alone, why'd she come here, of all places?

Well, that was his job, right? To find out.

He opened the door and set the cups down on his desk. "Good morning. Sorry you had to wait so long."

She nodded stiffly without altering her wary posture. He wondered where all that tension was coming from.

He extended his hand. She glanced at it, then at his face—damn, he wished he could see her eyes—and then at the foam cups.

"Is one of those for me?" she asked softly.

After a moment, he lowered his hand. He gave her one of the cups, thinking police station coffee was unlikely to improve her mood any. She accepted it without removing her gloves, her other arm still hugging her midsection. Her voice was soft, with a cultured accent that pegged her as an educated northeasterner.

He took off his trench coat and hung it on the rack next to hers. "Sugar? Cream? Well, not cream exactly, but we've got some kind of white powder that turns this stuff gray, if you want."

"Black is fine."

Should have known. He loosened his tie and unbuttoned the top button of his shirt. "I'm James Keegan."

"Yes, I know, Lieutenant."

Uh-huh . . .

She raised her cup to her mouth and blew on the hot coffee. Her lips were the only part of her face he could get a good look at, so maybe that's why he zeroed in on them. They were perfectly shaped, like the painted lips on a porcelain doll. If she had lipstick on, it was one of those dreary lip-colored shades. He wondered why women spent good money for colors that didn't look like anything, when for the same price, they could have a nice three-alarm red.

Seating himself behind his desk, he took a sip of his own coffee, and winced. *Damn. Should have blown on it.*

He pulled his little blue spiral notebook out of the inside pocket of his suit jacket. "The usual thing would be for you to tell me *your* name now. It's a custom we earthlings have."

A slight pause. He saw her swallow hard. "Jane, uh—"

"Doe?"

A faint wash of pink colored her cheeks.

With quiet authority he said, "If you give me a false name, I'll know it before the words are out of your mouth. Miss . . . Mrs. . . ."

"Doctor."

He sat back and allowed himself a small smile. "Mrs. Doctor."

Ah. Her mouth twitched, just for a second there. "Dr. Cook," she said in a resigned tone. "India Cook."

He plucked a ballpoint from the cracked Donut Hut coffee mug that served as his pencil jar and wrote *India Cook* and the date on top of the first clean page in the notebook. "I don't suppose you'd make up a name like that. What kind of doctor are you?"

She frowned at the notebook. "Do you have to write everything—"

"Absolutely. Now, would you mind answering my—"

"I'm a veterinarian. I specialize in cats."

"Really?" He wrote it down. "I hate cats."

"That probably means you've got something to hide."

He squinted into her sunglasses. "Excuse me?"

"A fear of cats—"

"I didn't say I feared them."

"—often indicates that a person secretly—"

"Speaking of hiding things, Dr. Cook, would you mind losing the shades?" She stiffened slightly. He gestured toward her sunglasses with his pen and said, "Take them off. Please. I like to see a person's eyes when I talk to them."

She hesitated just long enough to make him really curious. He began to wonder if she had a black eye—or maybe some kind of disfigurement. It was possible, what with the way she hid behind those glasses. A vague sense of guilt and trepidation gripped him as she lowered her head and slowly—very slowly—reached up, slid the glasses off, and settled them on top of her head. When she looked up and met his gaze, his breath caught in his chest.

Her eyes were . . . He'd never seen anything like them. They were incredibly striking, a heart-stopping coppery brown fringed with sooty lashes. Slightly heavy-lidded, they tilted up just a bit at the corners. Eyebrows like black brush strokes arched dramatically above them, disappearing into her bangs.

God, she was beautiful, sensationally beautiful. He hadn't realized, he'd had no idea. With those shades on, you couldn't tell, but now . . .

Was that why she wore them? So men wouldn't swallow their tongues every time they laid eyes on her? So they wouldn't gawk at her . . . the way he was gawking?

Suddenly self-conscious, he cleared his throat and looked away, realizing he'd maintained eye contact just a tad longer than Professor Mayhew—*or* Aunt Bridey—would have thought advisable.

"Thank you," he murmured. To cover his awkwardness, he bent his head over his notebook and wrote for a few seconds, then silently read it back to himself: *Most beautiful eyes I've ever seen.*

Get a grip, Keegan. He flipped that page over to expose a fresh one, then looked back up at India Cook and smiled in a way that he hoped would strike her as cordially professional.

She blinked, then returned his smile—for about a nanosecond—and then dropped her gaze. Noticing her coffee cup as if for the first time, she raised it to her mouth and took a sip, then glanced back at Jamie, and away again.

She was blushing.

This was getting interesting.

Too interesting. He had a job to do, and here he was exchanging flirtatious body language with a semi-spooky cat doctor who may or may not be here to provide him with information about a series of arson attacks that was seemingly both unpreventable and unsolvable.

Go for the no-nonsense approach, Keegan. Pretend she's . . . He smiled to himself. *Pretend she's Sylvie.*

He looked her straight in the eye, then abruptly looked away.

She wasn't Sylvie.

"Lieutenant?" Little lines of puzzlement formed between her brows.

"Dr. Cook?"

"Don't you want to know why I'm here?"

"Of course. I was just waiting for you to . . . feel comfortable enough to . . ." *Jeez, Keegan. This is embarrassing!* "I mean, I wanted you to feel . . . that is, if you have any information . . . about . . . anything . . ."

With one hand she nervously fingered the collar of her turtleneck. "I have information about a crime."

"A crime?" Maybe she *did* know something about the note. He fumbled in his desk drawer, came up with his little microcassette recorder, and set it for voice actuation. "Good. Great."

When he looked back up, he saw that her gaze was riveted on the recorder positioned in the middle of his desk. Her pupils contracted to tiny black pinpoints, making her eyes glow like newly minted pennies. Something had upset her, and you didn't have to be Einstein to know what it was.

"Look," he began, "I need to tape this—"

"Then I need to leave." She set her coffee cup on his desk and stood up.

"What? You can't just—"

"Are you going to try to keep me here against my will?" She snatched her coat off the rack and turned toward the door.

He stood and circled the desk. "Wait a minute. You can't leave."

He closed his hands over her shoulders just as she grabbed the doorknob. She gasped and flinched, then stumbled back into a corner, holding her coat in front of her like a shield. Jamie instantly raised his hands in a placating gesture, noting how her eyes registered a flicker of fear before she managed to compose her features.

Keegan, you idiot! Something had happened to her, something bad. No woman reacted this way to being touched unless she'd been victimized. Had she been assaulted? Raped? Is that why she was here? Mentally beating himself up for his lack of insight, he backed slowly away from her and opened the door.

"There," he said soothingly. "You can leave any time you want. I won't try to keep you here, and I won't touch you again. I promise." Often in an interview or interrogation situation he had to feign sincerity; this time it was all for real. He felt ashamed, incompetent.

"Would you rather discuss this with a woman detective?" he asked.

Her eyebrows rose fractionally. "That won't be necessary."

Good. He wanted the opportunity to redeem himself. From the bottom of his heart, his only desire was for her to feel safe with him, to confide what had happened to her, to let him help her. He felt an almost personal interest in coming to her aid—curious, given that he'd just met her.

Returning to sit behind his desk, he motioned to her chair. "Please stay, then. You can put your sunglasses back on if you want."

She looked toward the door for a moment, then reached up and pulled the shades down over her eyes. Keeping the coat bundled in front of her, she sat down.

Jamie took a deep breath and let it out slowly. It would be a miracle if he could reestablish trust with her now, but he had to try. "Can you tell me . . . what happened?" With his notebook in his lap, he swiveled his chair around so that he'd be looking at the wall, and not directly at her. That should help.

"All right." He could hear the hesitation in her voice, and his heart went out to her. He kept his gaze averted. "It was a week ago that I noticed a new cat out back. I have this shed in back of my house, and when the weather started to get cold, I put a heater in there for the stray cats I feed. Anyway, I noticed a new one, a black-and-white shorthair. It looked like a tom, but I couldn't get close, because every time I approached the shed, all the cats would scatter."

Cats? Wondering where all this was leading, Jamie said, "Let's back up for a second, if you don't mind. Your house, where is it? Do you live in town?"

"On the outskirts," she said. "About a quarter mile from the roadhouse."

He glanced at her sharply. "Little Eddie's? The place that burned down last week?"

"Yes. My house is number four Crescent Lake Road."

He wrote down the address. "Have you lived there long?" he asked, thinking he would have noticed her before this if she had. Mansfield, although ostensibly a city, was really little more than a small town that had grown just a bit too big for its britches. He knew almost all of its residents by sight, if not by name.

"I moved in on the first of September," she said. "It was my father's house. I grew up in it. He died last spring, and left it to me."

He snapped his fingers, awareness dawning. "You're Henry Cook's daughter!" She nodded. Henry had defended a fair share of the bad guys Jamie had apprehended during his decade on the Mansfield police force, but that wasn't why Jamie had hated the man. The problem was Cook's personality. He'd been one of those self-righteous, my-way-is-the-only-way types who'd always kind of made the hair on the back of Jamie's neck stand up. When he'd died, Jamie hadn't mourned him.

But his daughter probably had. "My condolences," he said.

"Thank you."

He consulted his notebook. "So you moved here two months ago. Where'd you live before that?"

"New York for the past three years." She hesitated. "Newport, Rhode Island, before that. During most of the year, that is. We traveled a lot, and we had homes elsewhere."

We. It hadn't even occurred to him that she might be married. His gaze automatically sought out her left hand, but her wedding ring, if she wore one, was hidden under the glove. The disappointment he felt stunned him. My God, he'd only met this woman, and here he was, jealous as a schoolboy of some husband from Newport, Rhode Island, with "homes elsewhere."

He noticed how her gaze followed his to her left hand. "I'm divorced," she said.

He brightened. "Ah." *For God's sake, Keegan.* "I'm sorry."

"I'm not."

He stifled a smile and said, "Go on about the cat, if you would."

She fiddled with the strap of her shoulder bag. "After a while I noticed that he seemed to have a slight limp. Finally, yesterday, I managed to catch him. I brought him into the examining room—I practice out of my house— and discovered that all four paws and part of his right rear leg were burned. I dressed the burns and started him on antibiotics."

Jamie stopped writing and turned to look at her. "Burns." She nodded. "Are you sure? I mean, they were old wounds by that point—"

"Phoenix showed up a week ago, right after the road-house burned down."

"You call him Phoenix?"

She nodded. "Because he rose from the ashes. His fur was singed. He even smelled vaguely of kerosene. He was there at Little Eddie's when it burned, I'm sure of it."

"So this is what you came here to tell me about?" She nodded. So. She hadn't been assaulted, after all. Not recently, that is; from her skittishness about being touched, he'd bet there'd been some kind of victimization in her past. A lamentable situation—and all too common—but one which had nothing to do with the arson case. And that's what all his faculties had to be concentrated on right now.

She took a deep breath. "But there's more."

"Go ahead."

"I'd prefer...I'd prefer if you didn't write down the rest of this." To his surprise, she lifted her hand and slipped off her sunglasses, then looked him in the eye, imploringly. God, she was gorgeous. "Please," she continued.

"It was hard enough for me to come here. I kept thinking someone would recognize me, and find out . . ."

"Find out what?"

A pained look settled over her beautiful features. "I don't want to be the town freak, that's all. I just want to tell you what I know and then walk out of here and be left alone. That's all I want—just to be left alone—but I'm afraid if people find out what I'm going to tell you—"

"Dr. Cook. India." He adopted an expression of frank sincerity. If it was part of his detective's bag of tricks and not quite the genuine article . . . well, it wouldn't be the first time he'd had to play a part to gain a subject's trust. He just wished he didn't have to employ such artifice with this particular subject.

He stole a glance at the voice-activated tape recorder lying on the middle of his desk and saw the little red Record light go on as he said, "If you don't want me to take notes, I won't take notes." He deliberately closed up his notebook and returned it to his inside pocket. "Why don't you tell me what you came here to tell me? It's only the two of us."

She looked him right in the eye and actually bit her lip. He noticed her fingers twisted together in her lap and felt unnervingly like the big bad wolf. "Please promise me you won't think I'm crazy."

He smiled indulgently. "I won't think you're crazy."

After a moment's hesitation, she said, "I . . . sense things. I get . . . readings, if you will, off of people and animals, even inanimate objects. Psychic readings."

He just stared at her, his expression carefully neutral, although he felt as if he'd been kicked in the stomach. *Psychic*, for God's sake. She was telling him she read minds. Crazy? He *wished* he thought she was crazy.

Crazy, he could handle. Crazy, he could understand, work with, even sympathize with. But psychic? She had to be kidding.

She was, in a way, he supposed. Wasn't lying a kind of bastard cousin to kidding?

Why her? Why India Cook, of all people, with her ethereal eyes and her air of mystery and fragility? He'd found her deliciously intriguing. He thought back to Bridey and remembered the way she would reinvent herself for her more important scams, adopting a new persona carefully designed to push that particular sucker's buttons. Of *course* he'd found India Cook intriguing. He'd been meant to. She knew exactly what she was doing, this one, and she did it very, very well.

He rose, went to the door, and said coolly, "Thank you for your time, Dr. Cook. If we need to speak to you again, we'll get in touch."

Her eyebrows drew together just a bit, before she set her jaw and eyed him coldly. She put her sunglasses back on, but made no move to rise. "I don't like being dismissed, Lieutenant."

"And I don't like being conned, Doctor."

Her perfect lips opened and then shut. "I can't believe you're being such a Philistine about this."

"And I can't believe you've taken up such a big chunk of my valuable time—and yours—with this."

She crossed her arms and stared him down, a stubborn tilt to her head. "I do have psychic powers, Lieutenant. I've had them for three years. Also as a child for a while—"

"Dr. Cook, you picked the wrong detective to come to with this tale."

"You're the detective in charge of the arson case. I read it in the *Mansfield Courier*."

"And I'm the detective who will never, while there's a sun in the sky and fish in the sea, *ever* believe a word of all this."

"Why not?" she challenged.

Careful. "I have my reasons." He gestured toward the door. "Now, if you'll please—"

"Fine. I don't need this." She rose and crossed to the open doorway, then stopped abruptly and stood with her back to him. After a moment, she shook her head almost imperceptibly. "I can't do this. I can't just walk out without telling you what I know. If he sets another fire, and I could have done something to stop it..." She turned, took her seat again, and lifted her chin. "Five minutes. Just hear what I have to say, then I'll leave. Believe me, I can't wait to get out of here."

He sighed heavily, then sat down behind his desk and waved a hand toward her as if to say, *Go ahead.*

She licked her lips, normally an indication of nervousness. Was she worried that she hadn't rehearsed her part well enough? Or maybe she just figured the sight of her pointed little tongue flicking out to moisten those china doll lips might get under his skin, just a little, might make him start thinking with his hormones instead of his head. Well, it wouldn't work. True, she was an attractive woman. Were it not for this little revelation about her "powers," he could see indulging in a passing fantasy about that nice wet mouth of hers...he might wonder if her lips were as soft as they looked, her tongue as clever. He might imagine kissing her, imagine how she tasted, imagine her tasting him and wanting more. She might unbutton his shirt and taste his throat, his chest, his belly, then reach for his belt...

"Are you listening, Lieutenant?" she asked.

He shifted in his chair, staggered by the speed with which he'd become so incredibly hard. *Zero to sixty in three seconds.* "Yes. Of course. You were saying..."

"That I experience two kinds of extrasensory perception. The first happens when I touch a living thing, a person or animal. I can sense their thoughts, even pick up visual images of the things they see or have seen. That's telepathy. The second is when I get a reading off of an inanimate object. Those readings are much less refined, just leftover energy from whoever touched the object before me. That's—"

"Psychometry," Jamie supplied.

A heartbeat's pause. "Yes. You know about psychic phenomena?"

"Oh, yes," he said sarcastically, arousal waning swiftly. "I know all about it."

She studied him for a second and then went on. "When I first touched Phoenix, to capture him, I got an instant image of flames leaping up all around him. I felt his terror, his helplessness. Later, as I was cleaning and dressing his burns, I saw a man's face—young, with dark hair. And there was some kind of basement or workroom in an old brick building, with strange wrought iron railings on the stairs—but that's not what was on fire."

A gust of laughter escaped him. "You got all that from a cat?"

She squared her shoulders. "They *were* unusually powerful readings, very detailed. Intense emotions create the strongest energy. And I was especially susceptible to Phoenix's terror. I'm... a little phobic about fire. More than a little. When I was five, I was trapped in a burning barn. I've had nightmares about it ever since. It's probably my strongest fear, and it's exactly what Phoenix experienced at the roadhouse."

Jamie stood up. "Thank you again, Dr. Cook, for coming in to make this report."

"I'd recognize him again," she said. "The young man with dark hair. I'd know that face anywhere. Shouldn't I look at mug books or something?"

Maybe she could bring the cat in, and have him look, too. "No, I don't think that'll be necessary." He stood by the door. "As I said before, if we need you, we'll call."

A few seconds passed, and then she stood up, reached into her bag, withdrew a business card, and handed it to him, careful not to touch him. "Not that I think you'll use it. Goodbye, Lieutenant."

After she left, Jamie picked up the little recorder, rewound the tape, and punched the Play button. He heard his own voice: *Good. Great.* A pause. *Look, I need to tape this . . .* He fast-forwarded. *That's all I want . . .* Her voice. *Just to be left alone . . . but I'm afraid if people find out what I'm going to tell you . . .*

She had *that* right.

"INDIA COOK! Is that you?"

Pausing with her hand on the front door, India turned to see Sam Garrett striding toward her through the sea of activity that was the Mansfield police station. She should have known he'd recognize her if he saw her, despite the shades. During her high school years, his daughter, Miranda, had been India's best friend. They'd been inseparable, and India had practically lived at the Garrett household. Yet she'd seen the captain only twice since leaving for college fifteen years ago—at her lavish Newport wedding, and then at her father's funeral here in Mansfield last May. On neither occasion had they had the chance to talk.

"Captain Garrett, how are you?"

He extended his hand, but she pretended to busy herself with taking off her sunglasses and fumbling in her shoulder bag to find their case.

"It's 'Sam,'" he corrected genially. "And I'm just great. I'm retiring in five months, three weeks and four days."

She smiled. "Are you finally going to write that book? What is it—?"

"*Zen and the Art of Bass Fishing*? Absolutely! What about you? Still filthy stinking rich?"

"Uh . . . actually, it was Perry who was filthy stinking rich. Thanks to his clever little prenuptial agreement, he's just as rich as ever, and I'm clipping coupons. Nothing left but my dignity."

He looked somewhat abashed. "Sorry, kid. Miranda didn't say anything."

"I guess she doesn't know. I haven't seen her since the wedding." She took a deep breath. "Perry and I didn't even make it to our first anniversary, Sam. I left him three years ago. I've been in New York since then, working at an animal hospital."

"So are you back in town to settle up the estate?"

"Actually, I . . . I kind of live here now. I moved into Dad's house a couple of months ago. Turned the front parlor and study into a waiting room and examining room and set up a practice."

He frowned. "And you didn't look me up?"

She shrugged self-consciously. "I keep a low profile, Sam."

Sam nodded slowly. "Fair enough. So. What brings you to my humble place of business this morning?"

India hesitated, wondering how much to tell him. She remembered what a great father she'd always thought he was, the perfect person to raise a teenager—firm, but fair, with a healthy appreciation for adolescent eccentrici-

ties. He'd always understood when they got weird on
him.

Drawing a steadying lungful of air, she filled in some
of the blanks from the past four years . . . the lightning,
the strange powers that changed her life . . . and finally
Phoenix and the shadowy face she saw when she touched
him.

Sam just stared at her, and for a few uneasy moments
she feared that he might show her to the door, as had the
skeptical Lieutenant Keegan. But then he grinned and
said, "Tell you what. Just for the hell of it, why don't we
go on over and sit you down with some mug shots? How
would that be?"

She blinked. "Really?"

An idle shrug. "What have we got to lose? Long as you
got the time—" he motioned her to follow him "—and
you don't mind . . ."

"Mind? That's why I came here."

A minute later he had her sitting at a big table outside
his office, poring over mug books. No snide laughter, no
funny looks, just "See if you can find a face that looks like
the one you saw."

Good old Sam Garrett, she thought as she settled in
and began flipping pages. If only her own father had been
half as understanding, half as capable of accepting her
for who she was, idiosyncrasies and all.

She conjured up in **her** mind the face she sought in the
mug shots—young, good-looking in a street-punk kind
of way, black hair, and dark, intense eyes. There were
hundreds of pictures in the mug books, and she scruti-
nized every one that might remotely have been a match,
but after a while she began to think it was a waste of time.
The faces began to blur together, to take on the same
distinctive features, to look like . . .

Lieutenant Keegan.

She sat back and rubbed her eyes, but that only crystallized his image in her mind. Despite her ambivalence—correction, antipathy—toward him, she had to admit that he had a remarkable face. Like the rest of him, it was big, with a broad forehead, a solid chin, and an almost too perfect Roman nose. He had dark, overgrown hair that tended to spill onto his forehead, and one of those mouths that always looked as if it were about to break into a boyish grin.

That navy blue suit of his was nothing special, at least as compared to the ones her husband had had custommade in Milan. Perry had always taken great pains to have the tailor pad the shoulders and taper the seams just so, in order to achieve the commanding, athletic look he admired, but which nature had denied him.

Nature had not been so stingy with James Keegan. His very ordinary suit jacket hung flawlessly from massive shoulders, emphasizing his tall, powerful build. All the thousand-dollar suits in the world couldn't have achieved the same effect with Perry.

But there was something more, something beyond his height and brawn, that invested him with a sense of authority and control. He had a way about him, a way of carrying himself that implied—no, proclaimed—that he was ready for anything.

He was the kind of man other men didn't mess with.

Women, on the other hand, were undoubtedly more than eager to tangle with James Keegan. Those beefy good looks, that deep, rough-around-the-edges voice with the slight Gaelic lilt, those midnight blue eyes with a hint of Irish devilment . . . He emitted an unmistakable buzz of sexuality that only made it harder to be around him—especially considering how exasperating he was.

Oh well. She rubbed the back of her neck and turned another page, thinking, *Just look through these books and then you can go home.*

Home, where she'd be completely, blessedly alone. No Henry Cooks or Perry Milbanks or James Keegans to deal with. No one to doubt her or ridicule her or lecture her.

Or, worst of all, touch her.

2

As soon as Jamie stepped onto the ground floor he saw her again, complete with gloves, sitting at a table outside the captain's office, going through mug books. She looked up at him as he approached, then retrieved her sunglasses from her bag and put them back on.

"You just don't give up, do you?" he asked.

"Lieutenant." Captain Garrett gestured to Jamie from the doorway of his office. "Would you mind coming in here for a minute?" Garrett turned, and Jamie followed him into the glass-walled room. "Close the door," he said, leaning on his cluttered desk and crossing his arms.

Jamie shut the door. "She's quite an operator, Sam. I made a tape, and I wrote a transcript from it of the really off-the-wall part, which you may find kind of amusing—" he handed Sam the blue notebook "—but there's nothing we can actually use." He turned and stared through the glass at India Cook's elegant profile as she flipped pages in the mug book.

"I want you to work with her," Sam said.

Jamie wheeled around. *"What?"*

Sam grinned and tossed the notebook onto his desk. "Lighten up, son."

"Lighten up? We're being had. Correction, *you're* being had. I want it in the written record for this case that I am unequivocally opposed to any assistance from that woman."

"What harm can it do?"

"What *good* can it do? For God's sake, Sam, we're not that desperate."

Sam dragged a hand through his hair and began to pace. "Yes, we are. Look, Jamie, this pyro nut job is gonna incinerate something else this week—and odds are, something bigger and flashier than last time—unless we can find him and stop him first. We haven't got a single clue to go on. All we've got—" he pointed through the glass "—is India Cook."

"When all else fails, call in the witch doctor, huh? I just can't believe you're falling for this malarkey."

Sam lifted his fishing pole from its resting place in the corner and hefted it in his hands. "'There are more things in heaven and earth, Horatio, Than are dreamt of in your philosophy.'"

Jamie sneered. "Oh, yeah. Quote *Hamlet* at me. *That'll* convince me."

Sam smiled as he fiddled with the reel. "I don't have to convince you. I only have to order you, remember? I'm still the captain . . . till April, anyway. Then it'll be your turn at the helm. But until then—"

"What makes you so sure they're going to offer me the job?"

The captain chuckled. "You're the golden boy of law enforcement in these parts, haven't you heard? Not only do you always catch your man, your man almost always ends up behind bars. You've got the highest conviction rate I've seen in my entire career, 'cause you never overlook the legalities. That proves you're smart and can think on your feet. Trust me, of all the candidates, you've got the best shot at the job." He took out his handkerchief, rubbed the pole where he'd handled it, and replaced it in the corner. "You want it, don't you?"

Words were inadequate to describe how badly he wanted it. Jamie tried to be cool, but in the end he just nodded and grinned.

Garrett punched his shoulder. "Then crack this arson case. That'll cinch it."

"I've cracked hundreds of cases. Why is this one so special?"

"Because Mayor Weems is coughing up a very major hair ball over this one. She doesn't much like the idea of Mansfield burning to the ground building by building. Not during *her* term, anyway. Keep that from happening and you'll make captain before your thirty-fifth birthday, I guarantee it."

"And if I don't crack it?"

The captain shrugged. "As you go through life, you'll notice folks tend to pay more attention to your big failures than your big achievements. Especially when they've got an important decision to make about you."

Jamie groaned. "I hear you. I know there's a lot riding on this case, and, believe me, I want to solve it. But that's exactly why I *don't* want to work with *the Psychic Connection* out there. I don't need a lot of voodoo hoo-doo gumming up the—"

"Lots of police departments work with psychics, Jamie. You know that. Even the FBI and the CIA use them."

"Come to think of it, I did hear something about there being a sucker born every minute."

"Well, then, you're looking at one of them," Sam said. "And as your captain, I order you to employ the services of India Cook in solving this case. Unless you've got some hot new lead you're working on."

Jamie sighed and shook his head.

"That's what I thought." He peered through the glass. "Looks like she's through with those mug books. Wait here, if you would. I'm gonna ask her to look at the third arson note, and I'd like you to be here for that."

"The third one? Does she know about the one that came today?"

"Not if you didn't tell her. And I'd rather you didn't mention it. I told her I want her to look at the most recent note. That's how I put it."

After a moment of puzzlement, Jamie grinned. "You're testing her, you sly dog. You want to see if her powers tell her there was another note this morning. You're not so gullible after all, are you?"

Sam rolled his eyes. "What is it about the Irish that they can make *sly dog* sound like a compliment? And no, I'm not gullible, just open-minded. To a point. I watched India Cook grow up, and I like her and trust her, but even so, a little proof wouldn't hurt. Consider this . . . an experiment."

Jamie couldn't repress the mean-spirited chuckle that rose from him.

"A friendly experiment," Sam added. "Meaning I'd like you to be civil. She's a nice girl, regardless of what you think. Try to get her to trust you. Use that famous Irish charm of yours."

"It doesn't exist. It's a known fact that seven percent of all Irishmen lack the gene for charm, and I'm one of them."

"You can't fool me, son. After ten years of working with you, I happen to know you can put on a pretty passable display of it when you want."

Jamie shook his head, wondering why Sam always got his way. *'Cause he's the captain, you moron.* Laying on his best Pat O'Brien brogue, he said, "I'll do me best, that I will, but I wouldn't be bettin' any money on it workin' with the good Dr. Cook."

"Attaboy." Sam left and joined India Cook at her table. She shook her head and held her hands up, apparently not having recognized any of the faces. Turning to look up at him, she removed her Ray•Ban sunglasses and shoved them on top of her head. Nice touch, allowing him a glimpse of those devastating eyes. They were the kind of eyes that could muddy a man's thinking, turn his knees to Jell-O.

She was good. Compared to her, Aunt Bridey was a rank amateur in the world of phony psychics. Bridey was always a bit too obvious, too greedy for publicity. Her flashiness tended to make people suspicious, especially the naturally doubtful policemen she tried to "help" in order to establish her reputation. India Cook, on the other hand, was smoothly, uncannily believable. Her feigned reluctance, her "I just want to be left alone" routine, was as slick a performance as he'd ever seen. Add to that her professional status—everyone trusted doctors—and he could understand, almost, why someone as normally astute as Sam Garrett might be taken in.

Yes, she was very good. During their interview upstairs, she'd actually had him feeling protective of her, empathizing with her. That business about not wanting to be touched . . . had that been a deliberate ploy to enhance her aura of vulnerability? She'd used that vulnerability—not to mention those amazing eyes and that sweet little mouth—to play him like the world's most gullible patsy.

It probably would have worked, too, had it not been for his own history, a history she couldn't possibly know anything about, despite her eerily perceptive observation that he had something to hide. She'd *better* not know anything about it. If the citizens of Mansfield found out about his misspent youth, he'd never in a million years make captain.

And he damn well intended to make captain.

Sergeant Albonetti brought Sam a manila envelope. Before he left, Albonetti frowned in puzzlement at India Cook's gloves, which was about as much expression as Jamie had ever seen him display. Perhaps, Jamie mused, he'd been too quick to draw conclusions about the shades and gloves and all-black getup. Perhaps they weren't symbolic shields at all, but indicators of guilt. After all, she *was* running a scam on the cops.

Sam motioned to her and they both joined Jamie in the captain's office. Jamie tried to think of something charming to say, but nothing immediately came to mind, and she didn't seem very receptive. In fact, she studiously avoided eye contact with him.

Of course she can't look me in the eye. I'm on to her.

Sam opened the manila envelope, withdrew two taped-together sheets of cardboard, and separated them, revealing a plastic sheet protector containing the original of the first arson note. Handing it to Dr. Cook, he said, "This is the note, India. Do you need me to take it out of the protector?"

"No, I can get readings through plastic, if it's thin enough. This should be fine." She removed her gloves and laid them on Sam's desk, then held the plastic-clad note between her palms, her eyes unfocused, her brows drawn together in a show of concentration. She shook her head slightly. "Inanimate objects yield very crude readings," she said.

How convenient.

"But," she continued, "I'm getting quite a bit off of this. It's probably because the person who sent it had to handle it a lot to paste all these letters down. The more an object has been handled by someone, the stronger their lingering vibrations are. I think—" she frowned and scrunched up her face "—I think I'm picking up on this guy's thought processes as he worked on this note. He was thinking about the fires he'd set so far, about their being... unimportant, incidental. He only set them to serve some... larger purpose, some final goal." She relaxed her face and looked at Sam. "Does that make any sense?"

Jamie rolled his eyes. Every gypsy fortune-teller worth her bangle bracelets knew that trick. You fed your mark something general and then started asking questions, leading him into revealing more and more—then you turned around and fed his own revelations back to him in the form of a "psychic reading." If it was done well, nine pigeons out of ten went along with it and never suspected they'd been had.

Sam maintained a studiously blank expression—perhaps, thought Jamie, because he saw through her ruse, or perhaps because the Firefly's "larger purpose" was just as much a mystery to the police as it was to India Cook. "Go on."

Dr. Cook closed her eyes. "It won't end with the roadhouse. I'm sure of that. This man—it's a man—intends to repeat this crime, to send more notes and burn down more buildings."

"Can you tell anything about him?" Sam asked.

"I sense... arrogance. Extreme arrogance. But nothing concrete. No physical description, nothing like that."

Nothing concrete, thought Jamie. *Surprise, surprise.*

"What I *can* tell you," she continued, "is that each fire will be bigger than the last. It's all leading up to something. Something big." Shuddering, she opened her eyes and shook her head. "One final, devastating blaze."

She let out a quivering breath and handed the note back to Sam. "His plan is to set a fire every week. I'm sure he's already mailed a fourth note by now."

Sam nodded. "It arrived this morning."

Her eyes widened and then narrowed. "I don't like being tested, Sam. Especially with no warning."

"It was very ungallant of me," the captain said. "I apologize. I'm impressed that you knew about the fourth note, though." He turned to Jamie. "What do you think now, son?"

Jamie snorted derisively. "I think we were due for another note, as everyone in this town—including Dr. Cook here—was very well aware." He shrugged and added, "Maybe she even overheard the guys at the front desk talking about it when she came in this morning."

She drew herself up. "No, Lieutenant. I overheard nothing."

Sam said, "The lieutenant doth protest too much, methinks."

"Which means?" Jamie prompted.

"Which means part of the reason you're such a crackerjack detective is your own blue sense. Cop ESP," he explained to Dr. Cook.

"I do not have—"

"Then how do you explain the time you were driving by that 7-Eleven store and 'just got the feeling' something was going on inside, and went back and stopped a robbery in progress? Or the time that old woman disappeared and you knew to look—"

"Hunches," Jamie said.

"Another word for the blue sense."

Jamie waved a hand in dismissal. "It's deductive reasoning," he insisted. "On a subconscious level. Without realizing it, you piece together subliminal clues. Everyone who does our kind of work on a daily basis develops that capability."

"Not everyone," Sam said, "and not to your degree. I don't know why you fight this psychic stuff so hard, Jamie, but I don't want you to let your skepticism interfere with this case." He turned to India Cook. "For what it's worth, *I'm* inclined to give you the benefit of the doubt. And I'd be most obliged if you'd consent to cooperate with Lieutenant Keegan on this case. We can use all the help we can get."

She lifted one graceful eyebrow. "I've gotten the impression Lieutenant Keegan feels he can do very well without my help. Cooperation doesn't work unless it comes from both sides."

Jamie cursed under his breath. "Sam, this is—"

"Lieutenant Keegan will cooperate with you, India." Sam grinned. "He's a hardheaded pain in the butt, but he's smart." He pinned Jamie with his level, blue-eyed gaze. "Way too smart to start getting insubordinate at this . . . rather delicate point in his career."

Jamie speared him with a hostile glare, but Sam just laughed.

Dr. Cook lifted her coat from the back of a chair and put it on. "I don't know, Sam. I don't think it's going to work. I regret having come here. I've exposed myself to mockery, and the face I saw isn't even in your mug books."

How could it be? It doesn't even exist, thought Jamie. She should get an Oscar for this little display of resistance. It only made her seem more credible in Sam's eyes. This was one smart cookie.

"I'm not gonna be coy with you, India," Sam said. "We've run out of ideas on this case, otherwise we probably wouldn't be bothering you. As it is, I'd be most obliged if you'd consent to help us out. I'd consider it a personal favor, and I'd be in your debt."

She seemed to mull that over. "All right," she said. "But I reserve the right to quit the investigation at any time."

"Fair enough." Addressing both of them, Sam said, "The basement India saw in her reading had iron railings on the stairs with—what was it, birds . . . ?"

India nodded. "Little wrought iron birds perched here and there on the railings, as decoration. That's probably why Phoenix noticed them. Cats are drawn to birds."

Jamie tried to exchange a look with Sam, but the captain stubbornly avoided eye contact. "What else, India?" Sam asked her. "What kind of birds were they? Could you tell?"

She shrugged. "Just birds. I don't know. They had crests."

"Crests," Sam said. "Like blue jays?"

"Bigger." She squinted, as if trying to remember. "Like cardinals. They were cardinals, I think." Her eyes grew wide and her eyebrows lifted. "Cardinals!" She grinned. "They were cardinals!"

This time Sam did meet Jamie's gaze, his expression wryly curious, as if to say, "Do *you* get it?" Jamie shook his head; but then, he didn't quite get *any* of this.

"Lorillard Press!" India Cook exclaimed, with more animation that Jamie had seen her express all morning. "*Lorillard Press!*" she repeated impatiently. Jamie and Sam just stared at her. "You *have* heard of Lorillard Press," she added, sarcastically.

"Be a little strange if we hadn't," Jamie responded dryly, "seeing as how it's the biggest employer in town."

Sam said, "There's no connection to cardinals, though. They publish tax and accounting books, not bird books."

"You don't see the connection because you haven't lived in Mansfield long enough," she said.

"Twenty years isn't long enough?" Sam said.

"Lorillard Press was founded twenty-five years ago," said Dr. Cook. "Alden Lorillard quit his law practice, bought two vacant buildings in the center of town, and turned them into a publishing company. His warehouse used to be the old high school. And the building next to it that houses his editorial offices was—"

Sam snapped his fingers. "The Cardinal . . . something."

"Typewriting Machine Company," India supplied. "The Cardinal Typewriting Machine Company. I was seven years old when Alden founded Lorillard Press."

"Alden?" Jamie said. "You're on a first-name basis?"

"He'd been my father's law partner. They remained very good friends."

"Uh-huh." Jamie rested his hands on his hips and looked her in the eye. "So let me get this straight. You think the wrought iron railings that you allegedly saw in a vision from a *cat* are in the editorial offices of Lorillard Press because that building was once owned by a company with *Cardinal* in its name. And that this place with these wrought iron railings *might* have something to do with this mystery man you also saw—correction, *allegedly* saw—in this vision, and that said mystery man *might* have something to do with the arson attack on Little Eddie's."

Dr. Cook regarded him in stony silence, then turned to Sam. "Maybe the man whose face I saw works at Lorillard Press. Do you want me to ask Alden if he's got photos of his employees?"

"I already know he doesn't," Sam said. "Alden's always been, shall we say, a little behind the times in the way he runs his business."

"More than a little," she agreed, smiling. Jamie saw a fondness in her expression that sent an absurd little corkscrew of jealousy twisting into his stomach. "I saw him last week, and he told me he doesn't even have a computer over there—not one. Alden's a gentleman publisher of the old school."

"Sounds more like a dinosaur," Jamie muttered.

"Either way," Sam said, stabbing Jamie with a look of warning, "there are no photos to work from. That leaves only one option, if we want to ID this guy before he strikes again. You two are gonna have to stake out Lorillard Press in an unmarked car this afternoon from three-thirty to five-thirty, when the employees leave. Dr. Cook is to look for that face. Any questions?"

Jamie let out a long sigh. He said, "I'll pick you up at a quarter after three, Dr. Cook," then turned to leave.

"Lieutenant, wait," she said.

He swung around. *What now?*

"Isn't this yours?" Reaching toward Sam's desk, she grabbed Jamie's blue notebook with one hand and her gloves with the other. She held the notebook out to him, then pulled it back, frowning.

"What is it, India?" Sam asked.

Tucking her gloves into her shoulder bag, she held the notebook sandwiched between her bare hands. For a moment she stared at nothing, her mouth pressed into a thin, angry line. Then her gaze snapped back into focus and she looked directly at Jamie. Her eyes flared gold as those telltale pupils of hers shrank down to nothing.

"Slick move, Lieutenant, not turning the tape recorder off." She thrust the notebook toward him, and he took it. "I didn't realize you were quite that sneaky."

She knows about the recorder? With all the cool Jamie could muster, he slid the notebook into his inside pocket and smiled. "'Sneaky' is part of my job description."

"Thank you for warning me," she said stonily, pulling on the gloves. "From now on, whenever I'm with you—" she met his gaze for one brief, breathtaking moment, then slipped the shades back on "—I'll remember to keep my guard up."

She left.

Sam turned to Jamie. "Nice goin', hotshot. Next time I want a display of Irish charm, remind me to ask Sergeant Albonetti."

INDIA WATCHED from her front porch as the nondescript gray sedan made its slow approach up the gravel drive connecting her heavily wooded property to Crescent Lake Road. When it got close enough for her to see James Keegan at the wheel, she lowered her sunglasses—aviators this time—over her eyes.

He pulled up in front of the big stone and brick house, gave it a quick, curious appraisal, then leaned over to open the passenger door. "Dr. Cook."

"Lieutenant."

"Different sunglasses."

"Yes."

Those were the only words spoken during the entire drive into downtown Mansfield.

In a community of old buildings—the police station, the new high school, and a couple of fast-food places were the only modern structures in Mansfield—Lorillard Press occupied the oldest two. They stood side by side, both three-story redbrick buildings, recently connected by a second-floor walkway.

The two buildings shared a parking lot in back, surrounded by silver maples gilded in brilliant autumn foliage. The entrance to the lot, on Jefferson Street, was marked by a large sign announcing Lorillard Press, Quality Business Publications, and had an arrow pointing in.

Jefferson being a one-way street, Keegan was able to park along the curb directly to the right of the sign. He turned the ignition off and plucked the radio mouthpiece off the dash. While he reported his location to the station, India inspected him out of the corner of her eye. He'd traded in his suit for jeans and a denim jacket over a gray, hooded sweatshirt—an outfit perfectly suited to his disobedient hair and smart-aleck eyes.

It made her nervous sitting so close to him and having nowhere else to go. She tried to ignore the fact that he could reach out and touch her any time he wanted, tried to will herself to relax. She wouldn't think about his proximity. She wouldn't think about the fact that she could feel the heat from his body and smell the Ivory soap with which he must have recently bathed. The thought generated an image of him naked and dripping, which she promptly swept from her mind.

"This is a good spot," he said, clicking off the radio. "The trees and the sign provide cover. We'll be virtually invisible to people leaving the building."

India looked around. "What if someone arrives and wants to park in the lot? We're right next to the entrance."

"No one's going to be arriving this late in the day." He checked his watch. "It's almost three-thirty. From now till five-thirty, everyone will be going home, in fifteen-minute intervals, as their shifts end. They'll be leaving by the exit to the lot, which is around the corner on Main. No one will see us."

"What about the warehouse staff? They've got a shift that starts at four, don't they?"

He shook his head. "Not anymore. The second shift got laid off about six months ago. That's what happens when you've got a dinosaur running things."

He turned toward India. She shrank back as he got closer, but he was only reaching for something in the back seat, a brown bag. Any kind of casual physical contact, the type of thing other people took for granted—shaking hands, getting a pat on the back, even accidentally brushing up against someone—caused her mind to explode with bright, staccato images and riotous sensations.

Opening the bag, the detective withdrew two bottles of mineral water and offered one to India, shrugging. "It's all I had in the fridge at home. That and a six-pack of Harp's, but I'm on duty—such as it is."

She accepted the drink and let him open it for her. It was pleasantly sparkly, and still cold. "Lieutenant, why exactly is it so critical that we not be seen?"

He swallowed about half of his bottle in one gulp. "Say you do finger some hapless Lorillard employee this afternoon. I could just take him in for questioning, but it wouldn't be smart. There's a legal concept called 'the fruit of the poisonous tree.' Information and evidence obtained from questionable sources—"

"Like psychics."

"Like psychics, is generally inadmissible in court. Therefore, I've promised Sam that if you make an ID, I'll tail the suspect home so we know where he lives. Then the boys stake out his house every night this week, follow him if he leaves, and apprehend him if he tries to start a fire. But if he sees us hanging out here this afternoon, he'll know we're on to him. He'll lay low the rest of the week, and we'll have lost our chance to catch him."

"But even if he does see us, he won't know who we are. We're in an unmarked car."

He drained the bottle, recapped it, and tossed it back in the bag. "Everyone in this town knows who I am."

She imagined that was true. He was the kind of guy who got noticed. His size, his personality and his profession would all tend to draw attention to him. Having spent four years trying to fade into the background, to make people leave her alone, India felt vulnerable just sitting in the same car with such a man.

He cocked his head toward a handful of people in the parking lot. "It's show time."

"What do I do?"

"Just check out the people who leave those two buildings. The employees who park in the lot, and that's most of them, will exit by the back doors within the next two hours, every fifteen minutes. If you see your mystery man, give a holler."

Most of the people in the lot headed directly for their cars, but a small group chatted together, laughing over something. All of the men looked too old to be the one she saw when she touched Phoenix.

India had to look across Lieutenant Keegan to see out the window, and she got the impression it made him nervous. He glanced at her a couple of times, stared out the window, then reached into a pocket of his denim jacket and withdrew his notebook and a pen.

"Can I assume I'm being surreptitiously recorded again, Lieutenant?" she asked, without diverting her gaze from the parking lot.

He looked at her, his eyes searching for hers through her sunglasses. Then a slow grin spread across his face. "You tell me. You're the mind reader."

"I have to touch people to read their minds."

"People—" he held the notebook up "—or things, isn't that right? Better keep your story straight if you expect this to work, Dr. Cook."

"If I expect what to work, Lieutenant Keegan?"

"This campaign of yours to enhance your credibility as a psychic by assisting the Mansfield police department in apprehending the Firefly."

"Is that what you think I—"

"That's what I *know* you're doing, Dr. Cook."

She sighed impatiently, keeping her gaze glued on the departing employees. "How do you explain my knowing about the tape recorder back there at the station?"

He chuckled. "You should work on your parlor tricks, Dr. Cook. They're amateurish. You'd seen me turn the recorder on and noticed when I didn't turn it off. But instead of calling me on it right then and there, you saved it up and used it to concoct a little demonstration of your powers."

"Sounds pretty calculating."

"It *is* pretty calculating."

She looked directly at him. "You don't know me, Lieutenant."

"I know you better than you think, Dr. Cook. And I suggest you keep your eyes on the parking lot so I can tell Sam we actually gave this thing a shot." He wrote something in his notebook. "And no, I'm not taping you right now. Happy?"

Before she could stop herself, she muttered, "Lieutenant, I don't know the meaning of that word."

From the edge of her field of vision, she saw Keegan turn and look at her, the curiosity in his gaze gradually softening. He opened his mouth as if he were about to say something, then seemed to think better of it, and returned his attention to the book. He wrote for another few minutes, during which the flow of departing employees petered out to nothing. "That's it for that shift, I guess." He tapped his pen against the notebook for a few seconds, and then asked, "Do you want to trade places?"

Sit on the seat he'd been occupying and have to deal with his vibes? "No."

"All right." He returned the notebook and pen to his pocket and leaned toward her. Again she automatically shrank back. "Easy," he said, groping in back for a thermos. "Care for some coffee? It's black."

Indicating the bottle of mineral water in her hand, she said, "I'm fine, thanks."

He unscrewed the cup on top of the thermos and poured himself some coffee, then became very still and stared out his side window, seemingly transfixed. She turned to look, and gasped in wonder, then took off her sunglasses for a better view. A gust of wind had loosened thousands of bright yellow leaves from the maples that surrounded them. They fluttered and spun against the azure sky like so many flecks of gold leaves winking in the sun. The dazzling spectacle held her captivated.

She realized he was staring at her.

"Beautiful," she said to cover her awkwardness.

"Yes, very," he murmured.

Nonplussed, she started to put the shades back on, but he closed a hand over hers to stop her. In the split second before she wrested out of his grip, she felt a powerful charge of desire shoot up her arm and rip the breath from her lungs. The TV in her mind flicked on and off, but not before she saw the eyes—her eyes—filling up the screen. They were...extraordinary. The most beautiful eyes she'd ever seen.

"Oh, my God," she whispered, her heart thundering in her chest.

"I didn't mean to scare you," he said. "I just don't want you to put those things back on. They, uh..." He glanced at her eyes and then at the parking lot. "You'll be able to see better without them."

India swallowed hard and nodded. "All right." *Yikes,* she thought as she folded up the sunglasses with trembling hands and put them away in her bag. *This guy's supercharged. Or maybe I'm just super-receptive to him.* That possibility did nothing to relax her.

Keegan sat in silence for a while, then nodded toward the parking lot. "Here comes the 3:45 crowd."

India turned her attention on the new wave of people leaving Lorillard Press, grateful to have a task that would take her mind off the all-too-potent energy emanating from Lieutenant James Keegan.

"Anyone look like your Firefly?" he asked, sipping his coffee.

She took a sip of water. "I don't even know for sure that the guy I saw *is* the Firefly," she said. "Nothing about the face screams 'pyromaniac.'"

"That's the problem with pyros. They don't tend to advertise what they are right on the surface. All we've got to go on is a psychological profile."

One by one, she inspected the departing employees. "What's the psychological profile, then? Why do these guys start fires?"

"For the thrill. That's part of what makes arson just about the most difficult kind of crime there is to investigate. Pyros tend to be wackos. Their motives just don't make sense to your basic well-adjusted police detective. Usually—" he glanced at her briefly "—it's a kind of a sexual thing."

"Ah." *Wouldn't you know?*

He took a long swallow of coffee. "They start the fire and then wait around and watch the crowds gather and the fire trucks come. The flames and the commotion are highly arousing to them. They get off on it."

"I see." Ridiculously, she felt her face grow warm.

"Sexual stimulation is the motivation for a surprising variety of crimes. You'd be amazed what turns people on."

She stared fixedly at the parking lot, wishing he'd stop talking about sex. It made her unruly mind speculate along paths she'd rather steer clear of. Unwillingly, she began to wonder what turned *him* on. What did Detective Lieutenant James Keegan find "highly arousing?"

Her eyes . . . the most beautiful eyes he'd ever seen.

"I never thought about that particular aspect of crime," she said, conscious of his amused gaze as he watched her scrutinize the lot. "It's very interesting."

The 3:45 crowd let up; people drove away. She sighed.

"No Firefly?" Keegan asked, screwing his empty cup back on top of the thermos.

"No Firefly."

From behind them came the rackety chugging of a car badly in need of a new muffler. India turned to see the battered, rust-speckled green T-bird draw up next to them, slowing to turn into the Lorillard Press parking lot. So. Brilliant Lieutenant Keegan had been wrong when he said no one would show up this late. She craned her head to get a good look at the driver....

...And gasped at the jolt of recognition. That black hair, those intense eyes...

"Oh my God!" It was the face she'd been looking for all day, first in mug shots, then here. It was the face she'd been fixated on, the face she couldn't get out of her mind, the face she'd seen when she'd touched Phoenix. "Lieutenant! It's him!"

She pointed to the T-bird as it slowly negotiated a left turn in front of them. Keegan's eyes grew wide. "I know that kid! That's Tommy Finn!" Hurling his thermos into the back seat, he yanked up the hood of his sweatshirt. "If he's seen me, I've blown it big-time."

Tommy Finn lowered his window as he pulled up to the entrance gate, then pushed a button on a control box and spoke into it. As the gate slowly opened, he reached up and adjusted his rearview mirror, looking this way and that into it.

"He's trying to get a look at us," the lieutenant whispered. Let's just hope he doesn't—" Finn turned to look back over his shoulder. "Damn!"

As Finn turned, so did Keegan, shifting in his seat so that his back was to the windshield. India couldn't figure out what he was up to until he reached for her.

She flattened herself into the corner between the door and the seat. "Wha— No!"

Suddenly his eyes were an inch from hers. "Sorry," he mumbled as he cupped her face with his big hands and lowered his mouth over hers.

3

SHE FOUGHT HIM, writhing and punching as he kissed her. Jamie seized her hands in one fist—she had no idea what became of the bottle she'd been holding—gripped the back of her head with the other, and threw a long, well-muscled leg over her lap, pinning her to the seat. He was strong; she could barely move, barely breathe...but she could feel.

Where their mouths met, she felt a hot sizzle of electricity. It crackled through her body, igniting her from within. She felt his strength in her own muscles, felt the effort he exerted to hold her still, saw the bright, shifting images that played through his mind like a TV scrolling rapid-fire through all the channels...her eyes, her lips... Tommy Finn looking back over his shoulder...

Can't let Tommy see me, she thought. No, that was *him* thinking that. These were James Keegan's thoughts flooding her brain, James Keegan invading her mind and her body as he held her immobilized.

Such warm lips...I knew they'd feel like this.... Was that her or Keegan? It was maddening, not knowing. She felt exasperated and frustrated and aroused, all at once, and she had no idea whose feelings were whose. He'd plunged his identity into hers, taken over her body and her mind, and the bizarre thing was, he didn't even know it! He had no idea how open and exposed she was, how vulnerable to this kind of violation. And it *was* violation, whether he intended it or not.

India whipped her head to the side, breaking the kiss, and gulped air. She felt herself—felt *him*—tighten his grip on her wrists and shift his weight so that he straddled her. Even as she thrashed wildly, she heard his mental warning to himself not to rest his weight on her; he was too heavy, he'd hurt her.

"Stop struggling," he rasped against her ear. "He'll think I'm attacking you." *Would Tommy Finn bother coming to the aid of a lady in distress? Would any of the Finns?* She knew that thought must be Keegan's, because she'd never heard of the Finns. "Is he still watching?"

It took her a moment to realize, through the blizzard of sensation that bombarded her, that he was asking her a question. She peered over his shoulder and saw Tommy Finn grinning back at them, the open gate ignored. "Y-yes, but—"

"Then we'd better give him a good show." His mouth met hers again, this time more gently. *Take it easy...she's scared.* Little burning sparks, like static electricity, tickled her as he pressed his lips to hers. The warmth of the kiss spread through her entire body. Her hands relaxed; he loosened his grip experimentally—*She's not fighting me anymore*—then took her arms and wrapped them around his back. *Might as well make this look real.*

It is real, she thought—he thought?—as his big hands tangled in her hair, his lips moving over hers with a slow, deliberate sensuality that took her breath away. *I've wanted this all day.* She *had* wanted this all day, she realized, ever since this morning in his office.... *Ever since she took those sunglasses off the first time....*

Her mental TV clicked on and she saw them again, her eyes, golden and translucent, mysterious and knowing. *The most beautiful eyes I've ever seen.* She saw more then, in luminous black-and-white: her china doll lips, her pale hands, the shape of her breasts beneath her black sweater. She imagined what they would feel like, cupped in her hands—*his* hands! Would they be as soft as they looked? Was she wearing a bra? Would he be able to feel their warmth through the sweater?

He couldn't touch her there—he could barely justify kissing her, could never justify *that*—but God, he wanted to. His hands itched to slide up under that sweater and feel her bare skin against his palms, fill his hands with her. He imagined how her breasts would feel, weighty and soft, the skin like hot satin. He could almost feel the sensitive nipples responding to his touch, tightening....

India was mesmerized. This was her he was thinking about, her he wanted to touch so intimately. In her mind's eye she saw a breast, just one, pale and perfect, saw a hand close over it with exquisite tenderness. No man had touched her since Perry—and Perry had never touched her like that, so carefully, as if she were a precious thing, a thing of value.

She felt a warmth and heaviness in her lower body— *his* lower body—as his hunger uncoiled there, felt his aching flesh stiffen and rise, straining at the button fly of his jeans. Despite her anxiety, India couldn't help but marvel at this remarkable new sensation. So this was what it felt like to get an erection! She felt his mind focus on the throbbing pressure between his legs; he wanted to press it against her, grind himself into her, relieve the unbearable pressure.

Back off, back off!

That was him, not her. A warning to himself, a command. Shaken, he pulled away from her, yanking his sweatshirt down—*Don't let her see*—and said, a little breathlessly, "Is he gone?"

Swallowing hard, India looked at the gate, which was closed. No T-bird. "Yes."

He nodded—*Better play this cool*—then levered himself off of her and folded his big body back into the driver's seat.

"Oh," he said, reaching down and retrieving India's bottle of mineral water, which had rolled onto the floor and soaked the worn rug beneath her feet.

"Sorry," India said.

"No, I'm sorry," he said, tossing the bottle in back and turning the key in the ignition. "I'm . . ." He shook his head, frowning. "Sorry. You understand it was just . . . it didn't mean anything. I was just trying to hide my face from—"

"I understand," India said.

"All right. Good." He put the car in gear and pulled away from the curb. India thought about the kiss, and his excuse for it, as he drove in silence. He had no idea, of course, how transparent that excuse was. The kiss, even if it had started as a simple ruse, had quickly become much more than that. Clearly, he intended to pretend it had been business as usual, not knowing how pointless it was to lie to a woman who could read his mind . . . and feel exactly what he felt.

India toyed with, and rejected, the notion of calling his bluff, repeating his own thoughts and feelings back to him as proof of her powers. For one thing, it would seem as if she were ridiculing his attraction to her, and she found that, despite her ambivalence toward him, she just couldn't be that much of a bitch. For another. . . well, he'd already told her that he would never, "while there's a sun in the sky and fish in the sea," believe in her psychic powers. Indeed, he had dismissed her two displays of it—

her knowing about the fourth arson note and the tape recording—as amateurish parlor tricks.

India doubted there was any proof he would find convincing. She had learned long ago that, if someone was determined not to believe, no demonstration, no matter how amazing, would make a difference. And Detective Lieutenant James Keegan seemed steadfastly determined not to believe.

"Thought I'd take you on a little detour," he said, tilting his head toward the side window. "A little tour of West Bonesteel, one of Mansfield's more humble avenues."

Why's he doing this? she thought, looking out at the neighborhood of dilapidated old houses with peeling paint jobs and badly patched roofs.

"That's the Finn place," he said, pointing as he drove by at about five miles an hour.

The house was large, and remarkably ugly. What little paint still clung to its ragged shingles was Pepto-Bismol pink, and its rambling porch had collapsed to the ground in several places. Half a dozen vehicles—some on blocks, some not—littered a yard devoid of grass. A swarm of stick-wielding children chased a pack of skinny dogs into the backyard as they passed.

"Tommy Finn lives there?" India asked.

"Him and about twenty other Finns."

"Twenty?"

Keegan shrugged as he turned the corner and picked up speed. "Maybe more. It's an extended family situation, and I'll be damned if I can keep track of the buggers. They're in and out of the slammer a lot, and they reproduce like cockroaches. Right now, I believe we've got about four generations in residence, though. There's maybe half a dozen males around Tommy's age—in their twenties, most of them—all cousins, and all trouble of one sort or another from the day they were spawned."

"Including Tommy, I take it."

"Actually, out of the whole godforsaken lot of them, Tommy's the only one who's ever bothered to hold down an honest job. About six months ago, he started doing janitorial work at Lorillard—four to midnight—and he's kept his nose clean the whole time."

"Six whole months?" India said sarcastically.

"That's a lot for a Finn. I'm not making him out to be some kind of angel. God knows he got in enough scrapes while he was growing up. Boosted a few cars, dealt a little grass." He chuckled. "But he's a slippery son of a bitch. We never did manage to catch him red-handed."

India studied Keegan's profile as he drove: the stubborn jaw, the flash in his eyes. "You sound as if you admire Tommy Finn," she said.

He seemed to consider that. "I don't know. Takes a certain talent to live on the edge of the law for years and manage to avoid arrest. It's no sin to admire talent, no matter what form it takes."

India nodded thoughtfully. Keegan felt a kinship with Tommy. Interesting. "Your point, Lieutenant?"

He drew in a deep breath and glanced warily at her before returning his gaze to the road. "My point is, Tommy Finn, for whatever reason, seems to be trying to clean up his act. Right now he's one less Finn for the Mansfield Police Department to worry about. Or was, until you fingered him as the Firefly. Now I'm going to have to order patrolmen who could be doing something useful to stake out the Finn place every night this week just to satisfy—"

"I never said he was the Firefly!" India protested. "I just said I—"

"Saying he's the guy you saw in your vision pretty much amounts to the same thing, Dr. Cook. Now, what I'm saying is, the kid has gone straight. I don't know why, and I honestly don't care." Anger had thickened his Irish accent, India noted. "I also don't really care why you happened to pick Tommy Finn out of all the petty criminals in Mansfield to be the scapegoat in this little charade of yours—"

"Scapegoat!"

"What I'm saying is, I'm not going to let you crucify a man who's very likely innocent just to serve your own—"

"Crucify!"

"You're playing with people's lives here, whether you realize it or—"

"Let me out."

"All right."

India swallowed her indignation as he pulled the car to the edge of the winding country lane and put it in park. Summoning a passable degree of cool, she got out of the car and slammed the door. "I'll walk home from here."

"Won't be much of a walk," he said, nodding out the window. "You live right there."

With some chagrin, India realized that they were on Crescent Lake Road. About twenty yards ahead, she saw the gravel drive that led to her house, and the mailbox topped with the little wooden cat-shaped sign on which was painted *India Cook, D.V.M.*

She leaned down and looked at him through the window. "Sam was right, Lieutenant. You *are* a pain in the butt."

"At least we agree on that." He drove away, grinning.

"WHAT'S THAT?" the little girl exclaimed as India inserted the needle into the vial.

"Jessica," her mother scolded, "let the doctor work."

"That's all right." India smiled reassuringly as she drew the feline rabies vaccine into the syringe. "It's medicine to keep Gus from getting sick." The child bit her lip. "Don't worry, Jessica," she said as she deftly administered the shot on the animal's back. "See? He didn't feel a thing."

"Wow!"

"Now let's see how much this big boy weighs." As India lifted the complacent Persian onto the scale, she heard the outer door to the waiting room open, and wondered who it was, Gus being her first, last, and only appointment that morning.

"Just have a seat," she called through the open door of the examining room, wishing, not for the first time, that she could afford a receptionist. "I'll be with you in a—"

She gasped as a dark, imposing figure filled the doorway, then swiftly composed herself when she recognized James Keegan.

"Mommy, that man needs a bath!" Jessica observed.

"Do I ever," he agreed wearily. When he smiled at the child, India noticed dark circles beneath his eyes. He looked ten years older than he had when he drove away grinning yesterday afternoon.

He wore threadbare jeans, a blue New York Giants sweatshirt, and a gray baseball cap, all heavily smeared with soot. All in all, he looked completely filthy and a hundred percent male. As much as India disliked the man, she had to admit she'd never seen shoulders like that outside of a superhero comic book. There was something about all that masculine brawn that made her feel just slightly giddy—as if she couldn't decide whether to run and hide or stay and . . . what? Wrestle him to the ground? Entice him to wrestle her?

Stop it! she scolded herself. *This is James Keegan. You don't like him, remember?* Besides, how could she think about "wrestling" with a man when she couldn't even bear to be touched? Speaking of which, why, after managing to go four years without giving a second thought to any man, had she picked *this* one to start getting hung up on?

The sharp odor of woodsmoke clung to him, prompting Jessica to add a disgusted "Pee-you!" to her assessment.

"I heard about the fire on the news this morning," India said as she heaved Gus off the scale and settled him back onto the examining table. "McGill's Hardware and Lumber?"

He took off his cap and stuffed it in a back pocket of his jeans. "Now it's just McGill's Hardware. The lumberyard's a smoking pit."

"Were you there all night?" she asked as she wrote Gus's weight on his chart.

"Me and the state fire investigator. Since 2:20 a.m., when the alarms sounded. Listen, uh . . . if you have a minute, there's something I'd like to show you." He held up a small metal can on which was taped a white tag with Evidence printed across the top.

"Sure, but I have to finish up here first. Why don't you wait for me in the kitchen? Through that door and down the hall. Help yourself to some coffee."

"Thanks."

Jamie blinked in surprise when he walked into the kitchen. It looked so . . . warm, so inviting, with its buttery yellow walls and sunflower-splashed curtains. He caught a faint whiff of new paint and realized that it was

India Cook, not her father, who had created this cheer-
ful room. Not what he would have expected from *The
Lady in Black*. Suddenly eager to explore, he left the evidence can on the brightly tiled kitchen table and wan-
dered across the hall.

Dr. Cook had not yet tackled the dining room, it
seemed. Table, chairs, drapes, chandelier... all were
coated with a soft, gray layer of dust, including a row of
framed photos on top of the china cabinet. Most were
enlarged snapshots of Henry Cook and Alden Lorillard
in hunting gear, holding up dead animals for the camera.

Most, but not all. There was a photograph of a pre-
adolescent India standing in front of a Christmas tree
with her father. The print had obviously been cut in half
to excise someone from the shot. Squinting, Jamie saw
the edge of a red dress. India Cook's mother? Jamie had
assumed, since meeting India, that her father was wid-
owed, it being unusual for a divorced man to retain custody, especially of a daughter. But the truncated family
photo would appear to suggest a divorce—and probably not an amicable one.

Jamie's eyes were drawn to the last picture in the row—
a portrait of India, in a sumptuous wedding gown, pos-
ing between two rose-garlanded columns on the portico
of a mansion that looked vaguely like the White House.
He remembered having once watched wedding footage
of Elizabeth Taylor in her breathtaking twenties and
thinking it couldn't get any better than that. But that was
before he'd seen India Cook in white satin and beaded
lace, her jet hair crowned with lilies, her perfect lips
curved in an enigmatic smile, her hypnotically beautiful
eyes gazing straight through the camera at him. Eyes like
that could almost make you believe in magic.

Or ESP. He shook his head. One thing he'd learned in his years on the force was not to judge a person's capacity for corruption based on his or her attractiveness. The most irresistible people could be the most unprincipled, and often were. Sociopaths, for example, although completely self-centered and devoid of conscience, were often extremely charming; they could make their victims believe almost anything. Not that he thought India Cook was a sociopath. But when he looked into those eyes of hers, he felt, despite his better judgment, a powerful urge to believe her.

It was an urge he would have to resist, with every ounce of his will. Because, as he should well know, it was all a show—a scam. But how had a woman like India Cook ended up running a mind-reading con?

Jamie left the dining room by another door and found himself in the front foyer. He hesitated only briefly before sprinting up the wide staircase. An enormous, sunny room beckoned him from the landing. Like the kitchen, it looked freshly redecorated, in shades of cream and ivory. Built into the back wall was an enormous stone fireplace, next to which stood a big, spindle-backed bed. Drawn to the stacks of small wooden boxes on the mantel, he swiftly crossed the room.

The boxes varied in size and shape, but they all looked old. He opened one, letting out a long, low whistle at what he found. Nestled within the felt-lined case were two antique guns with carved handles—*flintlocks*, he realized with astonishment when he noticed the powder flask, loading rod, and other accessories tucked into niches around the guns. A handwritten card attached to the underside of the lid read: "Pair of flintlock traveling pistols, William Smith, London, circa 1800. Original case with fittings."

Something brushed against his legs, and he flinched when he saw it was a cat—black and white. He took a quick step back. The animal turned and darted out the door.

"Good riddance," Jamie mumbled.

He opened more cases. There was a midshipman's dirk from 1805, a sixteen-bore flintlock sporting gun made in 1820 for the sixth Duke of Bedford, a Japanese wakizashi blade, several Indian thrusting daggers, an English fowling piece, circa 1725—

"Don't you need a search warrant for this kind of thing?"

Jamie wheeled around, an unopened brass-trimmed case in his hand. India Cook stood in the doorway, the cat cradled in her arms, both of them glaring at him. Her white coat was unbuttoned; beneath it she wore a black silk shirt and black jeans. Even her Keds were black. For the first time, he noticed the bandages on the cat's paws, and realized that this must be Phoenix.

He summoned a casual tone. "I'm not searching, per se. Just sort of . . ."

"Snooping," she interjected as the cat leapt from her arms and, thankfully, ran out of the room.

He adopted his most charming grin. "All part of my job description." She rolled her eyes. He killed the grin. "And I don't need a search warrant if I'm legally on the premises. You invited me in. That makes it legal." *More or less*, he silently amended.

"I invited you into my kitchen," she said coolly. "Not into my bedroom."

Jamie followed her glance to the bed. She hadn't made it up yet. A snowy white comforter spilled onto the Oriental carpet, and something lay carelessly tossed across the rumpled sheets—a scrap of smoke-colored silk, tissue-thin and edged in lace. Her nightgown? Absurdly, his face grew warm. A glance at Dr. Cook revealed hot color rising in her cheeks.

Jamie raked his mind for a way to change the subject, but he had a hard time banishing the mental image of India Cook in that whispery, translucent gown and nothing else. Finally he remembered the flat box in his hands, and opened it to find a velvet sheath with a horn hilt emerging from it. He concentrated on keeping his tone casual. "I wouldn't have pegged you as a collector of antique weapons."

She paused briefly, as if considering whether to pursue the issue of the questionable search. Apparently deciding to drop it, she said, "I'm not. My father was. He left them to me when he died. Alden's been looking after them. He gave them back to me last week."

"Are you going to display them somewhere?"

She shivered. "God, no. I can't stand the sight of them. They remind . . . that is, they're just so . . . I don't know." She shrugged carelessly as if to brush the whole subject off.

So they remind her of her father, thought Jamie, *and it's not a pleasant memory.* He read the card under the lid. "A Cossack dagger, eh?"

Something sparked in her eyes, and she almost smiled. "Ah, the Cossack dagger. Alden told me he used it as a letter opener. He didn't believe me when I told him I used to pick locks with it."

He laughed delightedly. "And you think *I'm* sneaky!" He unsheathed the dagger. The gold-inlayed blade was narrow and sharply pointed, but still . . . "You picked locks with *this?*"

"Actually, there was only one lock it worked on," she said, taking a couple of tentative steps into the room.

"The top drawer of my father's dresser. It had this enormous keyhole. You could have picked it with a meat cleaver."

Jamie carefully resheathed the dagger and returned the case to the mantel. "And what did this drawer contain that had the power to lure you to a life of crime?"

The pink on her cheeks deepened. "Nothing." He raised an eyebrow. "Nothing, just . . . books."

"Ah." He chuckled. "My da kept those books in a hatbox on the top shelf of his bedroom closet. Some magazines, too, as I recall."

She surprised him with a smile—a bit self-conscious, but disarmingly sweet. "So. Do you want that coffee or not?"

In the kitchen, India filled two mugs and placed them across from each other at the big table. "You take it black, too, right?"

"Uh-huh," he managed to say through a yawn as he took his seat. India realized how exhausted he must be after his long night at the arson site—probably hungry, too. She sliced off a hefty chunk of the banana bread she'd made last night and set it before him.

"Bless you." He ate the bread in about twenty seconds. She cut him another piece and he finished that off a little more slowly. Wiping his hands on his napkin, he said, "Tommy Finn never went home last night."

She sipped her coffee thoughtfully. "Is that right?"

He took a giant breath and let it out slowly. "I had a patrol car watching the house from eleven-thirty on. No Tommy. I don't know where he went when his shift ended at Lorillard, but it wasn't the house on West Bonesteel."

"Maybe it was McGill's Hardware and Lumber."

He frowned into his coffee. "Maybe. And maybe he went to some after-hours joint." He shrugged. "Or maybe he got lucky."

"Lucky?"

He met her eyes; a heartbeat's pause. "Spent the night with a woman."

"Oh."

"Can't base an arrest on maybes, though. Takes evidence to make a case."

India's gaze traveled to the can sitting in the middle of the table. "So are you going to open that thing up, or do I have to guess what's in it?" A galling thought occurred to her. "Is that it? Am I supposed to use my powers to tell you what's inside that can? Another test?"

He smiled tiredly and held up his hands. "Whoa. Demonstrations don't impress me, remember?" He picked up the can, unscrewed the lid, and gently tapped its contents out onto a clean paper napkin. "Don't touch it," he cautioned. "I sprayed it with lacquer, but it's still real fragile."

India leaned forward for a better look at what lay atop the napkin. It was about the size and texture of a dried maple leaf, but the color of pewter, and it smelled of ash and kerosene. "Burned paper?"

He nodded. "Part of the cover of a magazine. I found it near the fire's point of origin. Our pyro stuffed a whole bunch of magazines and newspapers under a skid of four-by-fours, soaked the lumber with kerosene, and lit it. He probably thought all that paper would just burn down to nothing, and most of it did. But I managed to recover this. Took me about four hours on my hands and knees with tweezers, and I just about went blind." He pushed the napkin toward her. "Can you read it?"

Peering closely, she saw that one edge of the scrap was less thoroughly burned than the rest. She could just make out, beneath the bubbled, silvery gray surface, crisp black type. "What does it say?" she asked, squinting at the tiny letters.

The detective produced a ballpoint pen and used it to point. "This section here, on the corner, is one of those printed-on address labels. This—" the ballpoint hovered near a letter "—is an *F*. This is an *I*. That's an *N*. The rest is illegible. Below it, we've got *S-T-E-E-L*, and most of the word *Avenue*."

"West Bonesteel Avenue," India murmured. "And the word above it is *Finn*."

"Bingo." He cautiously scooped the charred paper up with the napkin and slid it into the can.

India pointed at the container. "So, is that enough evidence to arrest Tommy Finn for the lumberyard fire?"

Keegan shook his head. "Just because that magazine came from the Finn house doesn't mean Tommy started that fire."

"But he probably did," India persisted.

The detective addressed her with a level stare. "In my opinion, Tommy is the least likely of all the misbegotten Finns to be the Firefly." India opened her mouth to protest, but he raised a hand and said, in measured tones, "I'm only going to ask you this once, Dr. Cook, and then I'll let the subject drop."

He leaned forward in his chair and drilled his gaze into hers. "Are you in possession of any significant knowledge, any clues or evidence, any information of any kind, linking Tommy Finn to the arson attacks?"

She held his gaze steadily. "Yes."

His eyes widened. "Yes?" He pulled his blue notebook out of a back pocket and flipped it open. "Would you elaborate?"

"I already have," she answered quietly. "I told you. I saw his face when I treated Phoenix."

"Not that," he said testily. "*Real* knowledge, *real* information."

India braced her hands on the table to help keep her voice calm. "It doesn't get any more real than that, Lieutenant. I saw what I saw and I know what I know."

He snapped the notebook closed and crammed it back in the pocket. "'I saw what I saw and I know what I know'? Sorry to break it to you, Dr. Cook, but that's not real likely to convince a judge. Or me, I'm afraid."

She nodded slowly. "Is that why you came here today? To ask me if I had some source of *real* knowledge of Tommy Finn's guilt? A source I'm presumably concealing by pretending to have had a psychic vision?"

"That's right," he said.

She rose. "Then I guess your visit here has been a waste of time, Lieutenant."

Keegan took the hint and stood as well. "Not entirely." He grinned engagingly. "That was *damned* good banana bread." He picked up the evidence can and pulled the cap out of his pocket. "I'll let myself out."

"I think I'd rather show you to the door, if you don't mind." She led him down the hall to the waiting room. "I don't want you ending up in my bedroom again."

"Would that be so bad?" Did she just imagine the subtle sexual challenge in his low voice? Was Detective Lieutenant James Keegan coming on to her? Or was he just being a smart-ass?

She opened the door for him. "Have a nice day, Lieutenant."

He settled the cap on his head and adjusted the brim. As he turned to leave, he said, "The nicest part of my day has just ended, Dr. Cook, but thanks for the sentiment."

Jamie had most of a day's worth of paperwork waiting for him at the station house, but first he needed to wash off all the soot. He drove back to his apartment—the third floor of a renovated town house in a quiet old neighborhood—filled the tub with scalding water, and settled in for a long, therapeutic soak.

Closing his eyes, he rested his head on the edge of the tub and sighed at the image his tired mind instantly conjured up: India Cook lying on that big white bed, wearing nothing but an ounce of smoky silk and that Mona Lisa smile. With a groan, he slid down until his head was submerged and stayed there until his lungs burned. He surfaced, gulping air and berating himself for his libido.

She was a con artist. A phony psychic. He wanted nothing to do with her.

He wanted everything to do with her.

Grabbing the big bar of Ivory soap and a washcloth, he began scrubbing off the soot.

He was supposed to work with her on the Firefly case, but that was pointless, of course. Her fingering Tommy Finn meant nothing, despite the evidence from the lumberyard fire. Either the whole thing was a coincidence, or—more likely—she'd deliberately picked as her scapegoat a member of a family known for petty criminal activity. All in all, her "visions" were much more of a nuisance than a help. They merely complicated a case that had already proven to be one of the biggest challenges of his career—a case that, according to Sam, had the power to earn him the captaincy... or snatch it from him. No, he could really do without the help of Ye Olde Gypsy Fortune-Teller on this one. Hers was a breed that brought back ugly memories, memories both of his own dissolute youth, and of the tragedy that officially ended it.

Yet Sam had ordered him to work with her. And he couldn't honestly say he relished the idea of cutting her loose. The fact was, he kind of liked having an excuse to spend time with her, fruitless though that time might be. If only she were genuinely useful to the investigation.

He set the washcloth and soap aside and sank beneath the water once more. By the time he came up for air, an idea was beginning to form....

He quickly showered and dried off, then went into the bedroom and grabbed his portable phone off the night table. Perched naked on the edge of his weight bench, he punched out the number of the *Mansfield Courier*.

"Sylvie, darlin'! I was wondering . . . do you still want that interview?"

4

THE FOLLOWING MONDAY, India Cook flung open the door to Jamie's office, whipped out that morning's *Mansfield Courier*, and slapped it down on top of the report he was writing.

He'd wondered what her reaction would be. Looked as if he were about to find out. "Good morning, Dr. Cook." His gaze rested on her tortoiseshell sunglasses. "Just how many different pairs of those do you own?"

A brief pause, and then she rummaged around in that big black bag of hers, pulled out two eyeglass cases, and hurled them onto his desk.

He picked them up. "Uh..."

"Wait." She withdrew another case from her coat pocket and bounced it off his chest.

"Whoa! Take it easy."

"I own—oh, I don't know—maybe a dozen? Maybe more. I've got them all over the place. You know why?"

He stood. "Dr. Cook—"

"You know why?" she demanded. She was shaking. Her face was pale, but her cheeks were crimson.

"Why?" he asked quietly.

"Because I like my privacy! I don't like people staring at me! I don't like people... *knowing* things about me! I just... I just want to be left alone!"

He circled the desk. "Look..."

She backed away from him, grabbing the *Courier* off

the desk and holding it up with a trembling hand. "Why did you do this?"

"This? The interview? Sylvie Hazelett had been bugging me for days—"

"You know what I mean." She unfolded the paper and read, her voice quavering, "'In an unusual move, the Mansfield Police Department has enlisted the aid of a reputed psychic, veterinarian India Cook, in solving the Firefly case. Says Lieutenant James Keegan, in charge of the case, "Dr. Cook has been enormously helpful in the investigation. She's given us invaluable information. Her powers amaze me."'"

She lowered the newspaper, took off her shades, and cocked an eyebrow. "'Her powers amaze me'?"

"Well..." He groped for the right words. "Perhaps that was overstating it just a bit."

"Overstating it? You think I'm a total crackpot!"

"Not a crackpot," he corrected.

"A charlatan, then. A...a..."

"Con artist," he said slowly.

She just stared at him. "If you think that, then why did you say this about how I'm so helpful and amazing? Why, for God's sake, did you tell all of Mansfield, New Jersey, that I'm a psychic?"

"Why should that be a problem? Isn't that what you wanted?"

Her jaw dropped open. "Wanted? If I'd wanted everyone to know, why would I have worn these—" she shook her sunglasses "—when I came to see you that first day? I distinctly remember telling you I didn't want anyone to know. I *told* you! I *told* you I didn't want to be the town freak, and here you go and publish it in the *Mansfield Courier!*"

Jamie studied her—her pinpoint pupils, the set of her jaw, her breathless rage—and felt some of his cocky self-assurance leak away. "Wait a minute. If you weren't after the publicity, why'd you come to the police in the first place?"

She threw her hands up. "To help you! All I wanted to do was tell you what I knew and walk away. But now, thanks to you and your smug, arrogant assumptions—" she waved the newspaper in the air "—everyone in Mansfield knows about me."

Jamie didn't know what to think. Could it be that she really did believe in her "powers" and was genuinely upset that he'd exposed her? Either that or her acting skills were even better than he'd thought.

She met his gaze, and it suddenly struck him that no one could fake the kind of pain he saw in her eyes.

"I'm such an idiot," she said tonelessly. "I really thought I could keep people from finding out. I thought . . . I thought you'd keep my secret. I thought I could have some peace here." She ran a hand through her hair. "Would you at least tell me why you did it? Why you said those things you don't even believe?"

He took a deep breath. "Because I thought perhaps the Firefly would believe them."

"I don't get it. Why do you care what he thinks?"

Jamie nodded toward the newspaper. "Did you read the part where I said you're going to search the lumberyard tomorrow afternoon for psychic clues to the arsonist's identity?"

"Yes. I take it you've got some hidden agenda?"

He nodded. "To smoke out the Firefly. If I can convince him that you really do have these powers, and that you're going to use them to figure out who he is—" he shrugged "—maybe that'll make him nervous. Nervous perpetrators do have a habit of returning to the scene of the crime, corny as that may sound. And crowds tend to gather when the police are investigating a site. I'm hoping people will come to watch you snooping around the lumberyard tomorrow afternoon."

"And you're hoping one of those people will be the Firefly."

"That's the idea," he said. "We'll take pictures of everyone who comes, and we'll be on the lookout for anyone who looks excited or . . . overly interested."

"I don't suppose it's occurred to you that this clever little plan of yours puts me in danger."

"You're in no real danger, Dr. Cook."

An exasperated little groan escaped her. "Just telling that nut who I am endangers me, Lieutenant! He may not like the idea that I could help identify him. Didn't you realize that?"

"The risks to you are minimal, Dr. Cook," he said soothingly. "Even if the Firefly buys into the whole psychic bit hook, line and sinker, he won't do you any harm. Pyromaniacs don't go in for assault, and certainly not murder, if that's what you're thinking. It doesn't fit their profile." He hoped. In his zeal to put his plan into action, he'd dismissed the potential dangers from his mind. But was he right to have done so? After all, it was India Cook's safety that had been compromised, not his own.

"Seems you've got all the bases covered, Lieutenant," she said frostily as she replaced her sunglasses. "Or most of them. Seems to me there's one small detail in this whole fabulous plan that you're taking just a *little* too much for granted."

He let out a long, dispirited sigh. "Your cooperation."

Her smile was completely humorless. "Bingo. And as of now—" she flung the paper onto his desk and wheeled around "—I'm officially off this case."

"Dr. Cook—!"

She slammed the door so hard, Jamie half expected the glass to shatter. He watched her until she disappeared down the stairs, and then let out his pent-up breath in the form of a virulent curse.

THAT EVENING, India rented Alfred Hitchcock's *Notorious*, which she'd never seen, and viewed it in bed with the lights off and a pint of Häagen-Dazs chocolate chocolate-chip ice cream for company.

She gasped when Cary Grant knocked over the bottle in the wine cellar and found it filled with glittering black metal ore. *Hurry!* she silently urged as he and Ingrid Bergman struggled to clean up the mess before her malicious Nazi husband, Claude Rains, found them spying on him. They raced upstairs and out the glass-paned garden door as Claude's shadow rounded the corner.

"Someone's coming," Ingrid whispered. "He's seen us!"

India sat perfectly still with the spoon in her mouth, heart tripping in her chest, as Cary pulled Ingrid into his arms. "Wait a minute," he murmured. "I'm going to kiss you."

"No, he'll only think—"

"What I want him to think."

Claude—and India—watched the kiss in stunned silence. The hesitant, impassioned caress of their lips, the ardent whispers, the eyes filled with desperate longing....

The phone rang, startling India. Gulping down her spoonful of ice cream, she fumbled for the remote and hit the Pause button. The image froze on the screen—a dramatically lit black-and-white tableau of *The Kiss* in extreme close-up. Cary Grant was in shadow, Ingrid bathed in silvery light. Their lips barely met; her expression was one of anguished desire.

Something about this scenario felt familiar, and as India studied the on-screen lovers, she realized what it was. Cary and Ingrid were doing what she and Keegan had done three days before, parked outside Lorillard Press. They were staging a kiss so that the onlooker wouldn't suspect their true motives for being where they were. But in both cases, there was an inescapable undercurrent of real feeling, real need, that couldn't be denied.

The phone rang again, but India couldn't tear her gaze from the screen—from Ingrid's half-closed eyes, glittering with passion. She recalled all too clearly the passion that had coursed through her as James Keegan held her in his arms and gave her the first kiss she'd had in four years. She had absorbed his desire into her, made it her own. It had been a novel experience, but also completely terrifying. Not knowing which thoughts and feelings were hers and which were his, had stripped her of her sense of identity, robbed her of any command at all over herself. She couldn't have felt more powerless and panicky if she'd been swept up in a tornado. All in all, a very frightening experience, and one she hoped never to repeat.

The knowledge that she must continue to guard against being touched filled her with despair. God, how she missed feeling the heat of a man's body, the feverish excitement of his lips and hands, the indescribable thrill of taking him deep inside. Before the lightning struck her, she had taken lovemaking for granted. Now that it was forever denied her, she mourned its loss.

Another ring. Her gaze locked on the screen, India tossed aside the remote and picked up the phone. "Hello?"

A pause. "Dr. Cook?" She recognized the voice immediately. Deep and virile, and just slightly Irish-flavored. "I'd just about decided you weren't there. This is James Keegan."

India studied Cary Grant's half-lit profile as her hand tightened around the container of ice cream.

"Dr. Cook?"

"Yes," she said, her voice oddly throaty. "Yes. Hello, Lieutenant. Um . . . what can I do for you?"

Another pause, followed by a low chuckle. "Have you been drinking, Dr. Cook?"

"What? No!" She lifted the pint of ice cream, as if he could see it. "I've been eating chocolate chocolate-chip ice cream!"

A gust of surprised laughter. "That explains it, then. I'm quite fond of that flavor myself."

India squinted at the luminous TV screen. "What can I do for you, Lieutenant?" she repeated.

"You can listen to me while I try to talk you into going to the lumberyard tomorrow afternoon."

"Lieutenant—"

"Just listen. Please. Hear me out." India said nothing, and after a moment of hesitation, he continued. "I know I haven't exactly handled this whole business of your involvement in the case very well. I guess I've been rude, and . . . you're right about that interview I gave Sylvie. I was out of line." Again he paused, and again India remained silent, her gaze riveted on Cary Grant's shadowy face. "You're not going to help me out at all on this, are you?" Keegan asked.

"No."

A deep breath. "I believe you when you say you really didn't want any publicity, and I'd like you to know that I'm sorry for forcing it on you."

"Does that mean you believe in my powers?"

A long pause. "I think it's possible that *you* believe in them."

"Right. Look, Lieutenant, I'm sorry, but I just don't see the point to my continuing with this—"

"The point is I need you," he said quickly, then added, "*We* need you. The department. For that matter, Mansfield needs you."

"But not for my powers. You refuse even to acknowledge them. You just need me to lure the Firefly into the open. You want to use me as a decoy."

"Look, this may be as good a chance as we get to identify this nut and stop him before he strikes again. Next time this guy burns something down, it may not be a cat that gets hurt—or killed. It may be a person."

India groaned. "Don't do this, Lieutenant."

"A child, even," he added, obviously realizing he'd struck a responsive chord.

"You're bringing out the heavy ammo, Lieutenant. What woman can stand the idea of a child being hurt?"

"I don't know of any." There was amusement in his voice. "Then you'll be there?"

On the TV screen, the time limit for the pause function expired, and the kiss came alive again. Lips brushed and parted and brushed again.

"Please say yes," Keegan implored, an edge of desperation in his low voice. "I really do need you."

On-screen, Ingrid Bergman closed her eyes, her head thrown back, overwhelmed by a passion that mustn't be—*couldn't* be—but was impossible to resist.

"You win, Lieutenant," India said, sinking back against the headboard. "What time should I be there?"

JAMES KEEGAN was already there when India parked her car on the edge of the big concrete lot in back of Mc-Gill's Hardware and Lumber at two the following afternoon. So were several dozen onlookers, congregated behind a barricade of yellow tape marked Crime Scene—Do Not Enter, which kept them about fifty feet away from the barnlike lumber shed—or rather, the charred remains of the half that was still standing. The rest was a blackened heap of ash and debris, and the whole thing reeked overwhelmingly of burned wood. Lumber that had been salvaged during the fire was piled in disorderly heaps around the shed.

The sun shone brightly, so for once, India wasn't the only person in dark glasses. Nevertheless, it was an unseasonably bitter day, and even her thick shearling coat couldn't keep her from shivering . . . until Lieutenant Keegan saw her and instantly smiled. The smile seemed so spontaneous, so sincere, as if he were truly delighted to see her. It filled her with a delicious and consuming warmth, despite the wintry bite in the air. She couldn't help smiling back as he beckoned her to join him in the cordoned-off area, glancing curiously at the cat carrier she set carefully on the ground.

"Thought I'd bring Phoenix," she said, unlatching the carrier's door and hauling out the reluctant tom. "That's a good boy," she soothed, enclosing him in her arms. Keegan took a step back, eyeing the cat warily. "You *are* afraid of cats!" she said.

"I told you before. I'm not afraid, I just don't like them. Why'd you bring him, anyway?"

"I thought he might be able to help."

Keegan frowned. "Help with what?"

"With what I'm supposedly here for—coming up with psychic clues. He seems to be an excellent medium for them."

He digested that for a moment. "Oh."

"I am perfectly well aware," she said levelly, "that you have zero interest in anything I might come up with today. I know that my true function—as you see it—is to draw out the Firefly. But, as *I* see it—" she shrugged "—why waste valuable time pretending to search for evidence, when I can actually do just that?"

"Then, by all means, search away," he said easily. "I trust you'll let me know if there's anything I can do to help."

"Well said, Lieutenant. I'm impressed." She glanced toward their audience, milling and chatting among themselves on the other side of the tape. "Half of Mansfield is here."

"I know," he said, scrutinizing the crowd. "It's a pretty mixed bag. Everyone from Father Kelly to Ginger Maxwell." India frowned in puzzlement. "Mansfield's only streetwalker," he explained, then pointed to a group of young men in black leather, smoking cigarettes and practicing kick-boxing moves. "That bunch over there are all Finns."

She squinted. "Is that Tommy? With the chains on his jacket?"

He shielded his eyes. "No, that's his cousin, Darrell." He signaled to a fresh-faced uniformed patrolman with a camera, who swiftly aimed and captured the group on film. "All the Finns look alike."

"Similar coloring. But Darrell's bigger than Tommy."

"And meaner." He blew on his hands and rubbed them together. "Of all those rotten eggs, he stinks the worst. You should have picked *him* to be your Firefly."

India drew herself up. "I didn't *pick* anybody, Lieutenant. I didn't even say the face I saw was necessarily the Firefly. I just—"

"I know," he said. "I worded that poorly. I seem to do a lot of that." He shrugged, his smile slightly amused, but mostly apologetic, it seemed. The frigid breeze whipped his tie and trench coat and tossed his hair into his eyes. India had an impulse to reach out and smooth it back off his face. One of her more idiotic impulses, she thought ruefully—for many reasons, not the least of which was that any touch, no matter how casual, would inundate her with his thoughts and feelings. But then she noticed the look in his eyes as he gazed down at her, and had to admit that it might, after all, be interesting to know what was on his mind at this particular moment.

"Keegan!" Turning toward the voice, India saw an elderly little lady in an oversize parka glowering from behind the yellow tape. She pointed with her cigarette toward the young patrolman, hovering nearby. "Will you tell this mouth breather who I am?"

"What's in it for me, Sylvie?" Jamie cheerfully demanded.

With a sneer, she growled, "I'll be your best friend."

"Don't threaten me." Jamie waved her in. "She's press, Billy."

Billy muttered something apologetic as he lifted the tape. The woman ground her cigarette beneath her heel and ducked into the restricted area, spearing the rookie with an I-told-you-so glare.

Keegan said, "Sylvia Hazelett, India Cook." India used her armload of cat as an excuse to avoid shaking hands. "Sylvie's the force behind the *Courier,*" Keegan told India. "And quite a force she is."

"Really."

Sylvie settled a pair of reading glasses on her nose and pulled a steno pad out of her pocket. "Dr. Cook, I was wondering if I could ask you a question or two before you start your—" she waved a bony little hand toward the blackened remains of the lumber shed "—séance, or whatever it is you're planning on."

India mouthed the word *séance?* at Jamie as the reporter located her pen. "Dr. Cook, have you always had ESP, or is this a recent—"

"Some other time, eh, darlin'?" Jamie settled a long arm around the reporter's shoulders. "You'll get your turn. But this afternoon, India Cook is all mine."

He smiled at India. *All mine . . .* She felt her face grow warm. Had he meant it the way it sounded? Something glittered in his eyes. He had.

"A five-minute interview," Sylvie cajoled.

"Sylvie, you harpy!" called someone from the crowd. India smiled when she recognized a grinning Alden Lorillard, his silver-haired good looks enhanced by a dove gray cashmere overcoat and silk scarf. "Leave the poor girl alone and let her do what she came here to do!"

"Shame on you, Lorillard!" Sylvie scolded. "You're a publisher! You, of all people, should support freedom of the press."

"I also support freedom from harassment." He lifted the tape and said, "May I?" to Billy. The young cop directed a questioning glance at Jamie, who nodded and beckoned Alden into the enclosure.

India said, "Alden, do you know Lieutenant Keegan?"

"Only by sight." Alden removed a kid glove and shook Jamie's hand. "And, of course, by reputation—and quite an impressive one at that, Lieutenant. It's a pleasure to meet you at last."

"Same here, Mr. Lorillard."

"Alden—please."

"Jamie."

Sylvie rolled her eyes. "Should I go mix up a pitcher of martinis, or does anyone besides me remember why we're here?"

"A séance, wasn't it?" Jamie winked at India. "What do you say, Dr. Cook? Are you ready to begin, or do you need me to fetch your crystal ball and candles from the car?"

India smiled and said, "I think I can manage without them this time, thank you."

"I'm not going to get that interview, am I?" Sylvie groused.

"It appears not, my dear," said Alden. "But you still have the pleasure of our company. That must be some consolation."

Sylvie snorted in derision. "Don't make me laugh." Stuffing her steno pad back in her parka, she added, "I'm outta here," and marched away.

For the next half hour or so, Jamie and Alden made polite small talk as they watched India—still holding Phoenix—pick her way gingerly through the inciner-ated remains of McGill's lumber stock. Her gaze seemed mostly directed toward the ground, although every once in a while she stopped and looked around, as if trying to get her bearings. Occasionally she squatted and touched some unidentifiable bit of debris, then frowned and shook her head as if in frustration.

Before yesterday, Jamie would have assumed it was all part of the act, an act he was all too familiar with. Now he wasn't so sure there *was* an act. Her outrage at being exposed as a psychic seemed too authentic to fake—so real, in fact, that Jamie had lain awake half the night before, grappling with the guilt of having been the instrument of her exposure. It didn't matter that her psychic "powers" were a product of her imagination. What mattered was that she evidently believed they were genuine, and that he had violated her trust and thereby destroyed the privacy that seemed to mean so much to her. He had, of course. That he hadn't meant to really didn't absolve him from blame.

"Cigarette?" Alden flipped open a box of Dunhill cigarettes and held it out to Jamie.

"I don't smoke, thanks."

"Good for you." The older man tapped a brown cigarette on the box, then shielded it with a gloved hand while he lit it with a match.

George Plimpton, thought Jamie. That's who Lorillard reminded him of—the looks, the voice, the refined geniality. Very much the antithesis of rigid, sanctimonious Henry Cook.

"So," Jamie began, "I understand you and Dr. Cook's father were friends for a long time."

Alden shrugged as he pocketed the matchbook. "Almost forty years. We shared a passion for hunting."

Jamie nodded, understanding the unspoken message: Alden Lorillard and Henry Cook hadn't really been such close friends. All they'd had in common was hunting.

"Then you've known India Cook since she was born."

Alden grunted affirmatively. "Funniest looking baby I ever saw. Pinched little face and hair all higgledy-piggledy. Grew out of it, thank God."

Jamie shielded his eyes for a better view of the subject of their conversation, running her hand along a half-burned beam. "How long has she . . . felt herself capable of . . . well . . ."

"She became telepathic at the age of twelve," Alden said. "Only lasted about a year, mind you."

Became telepathic. "Ah."

Alden regarded Jamie with a bemused glint in his eye. "Funny. From that article in the *Courier,* I gathered you put considerable stock in India's abilities. It would appear I assumed too much."

"I didn't say—"

"It's written all over your face. That's all right. I was skeptical myself, until the evidence simply became overwhelming. She sensed things—knew things—that she couldn't possibly have known by ordinary means. After a while, I couldn't deny the truth. The child had a gift, an extraordinary gift. A gift with great potential."

Jamie fisted his icy hands and shoved them into the pockets of his trench coat. "What kind of potential?"

"My God, man! Limitless potential! Unfortunately, Henry couldn't see it. I tried to convince him to use India to help pick juries. You know. Tell him which jurors would be inclined to side with him, and which with the prosecution."

"Is that legal?"

"Must be. I didn't invent the idea. It's been done for decades."

"You're kidding. What was Henry's reaction?"

"Oh. Well." Alden waved his cigarette. "He was outraged. Henry, you see, was rather . . . orthodox in his approach to the law . . . to life, for that matter. Extremely unyielding to new ideas and strategies. That's one of the reasons I dissolved our law partnership. He refused to take risks of any kind. But without risks—" he flashed a broad, white-toothed smile "—life would hardly be worth living. Henry could never see it, though. What's more, he never did believe in India's powers."

"He didn't? What about his wife? Or was this after the divorce?"

"During, more or less. Millicent left him that year. And no, she didn't believe, either. I don't know the details, but from what I can surmise, it was a horrible time for India, incredibly traumatic. Her parents' marriage falling apart like that, and both of them turning against her. They started off regarding her as a pathological liar, and ended up thinking her quite mad. No understanding at all—"

"Darrell, stop it!" wailed a high-pitched female voice as a commotion broke out in the crowd. Jamie turned to see that Tommy Finn had arrived on the scene. He and Darrell faced each other warily, surrounded by their leather-jacketed cousins.

The woman pleading with Darrell was pale, fragile, and very young, with enormous doe eyes and a fussing baby on her shoulder—Darrell's wife, Missy. Apparently they were estranged; Jamie heard she'd moved out of the house on West Bonesteel.

"You shut your face, you whore!" screamed Darrell.

Tommy fisted his hands. "Don't you call Missy a whore."

Darrell reached into his right boot. He flicked his wrist, and something flashed—a switchblade.

Damn. Jamie strode quickly toward the crowd, not pausing as he grabbed a short length of two-by-four from a pile. He saw the young patrolman reach for his service weapon, and yelled, "No, Billy!" The rookie backed away, looking confused.

As he neared the group, Jamie saw Darrell thrust the blade toward his cousin. "You shut up, too, Tommy! You stole my wife! Me and Missy were happy till you got in the way!"

"Happy?" Tommy held his ground, refusing to back down from the knife. Not smart, but Jamie had to give him credit for guts. "You think she was *happy* when you beat her up so bad she landed in the hospital?"

"She had it comin'! She wouldn't let me see my own son!"

"You tried to snatch him."

"He's my son! My flesh and blood! He belongs with me, not you!"

Tommy's hands balled into fists. "Come near Missy or the baby again and you're dead, Darrell! Dead! I'll waste you myself, I swear to God!"

Jamie ducked under the yellow tape and muscled his way through the circle of cousins. Darrell wheeled on him, slashing the air with the blade. He vibrated with rage, his eyes wild and unblinking. Jamie knew instantly that he was fried on crack; trying to reason with him would be pointless.

Darrell said, "This is family business, Keegan! Stay the hell out of it!"

Jamie held his left hand out, his right tightening around the piece of lumber resting on his shoulder. "Give me the knife, Darrell."

"You're on their side!" Darrell shrieked, slicing wide arcs in the air with the switchblade as he moved closer and closer to Jamie. "Go to hell!"

Darrell lunged, and Jamie brought the two-by-four down hard on his forearm. He heard the soft snap of bone. Darrell grunted. The switchblade clattered to the ground, and Jamie kicked it out of the way.

The young punk bellowed, more from fury, Jamie knew, than from his broken arm. He was too high to feel much pain, making him all the more dangerous. With his good arm, Darrell reached behind him and fumbled under his jacket. Jamie hauled back and slammed the piece of wood into his stomach.

Sucking in air, Darrell dropped to his knees, both arms curled around his midsection. He appeared to struggle for a moment, as if trying to rise, and then he fell forward, retching. Jamie used the lumber to lift the back of Darrell's jacket, not surprised to find a pistol grip poking above the waistband of his jeans. Tossing aside the two-by-four, he pulled out the little nickel-plated .32 semiautomatic, ejected the magazine, and racked the slide to open up the action. "You're a real genius, Darrell," he muttered, shaking a bullet onto his palm.

Ignoring the belligerent murmurs of the Finn contingent, Jamie waved the patrolman over and handed him the .32, then pulled out his handcuffs. "The thing is this, Billy," he said as he squatted down to shackle Darrell's wrists together behind his back. "If I'd have let you pull your weapon, first thing this maniac would have done is whip out that little auto, which, by the way, he's been carrying around fully cocked. Not a good idea to let an unhappy crack-head start squeezing off shots in a crowd."

"Sorry, Lieutenant," Billy mumbled.

Jamie stood and nodded toward Darrell's writhing form. "Read him his rights and take him to the hospital. I'll meet you there later."

"Okay, Lieutenant."

Jamie turned and saw India Cook and Alden Lorillard standing on the other side of the yellow tape. Dr. Cook clutched the cat tightly in her arms as she stared at him, white-faced.

India had viewed the altercation in dazed silence. Everything had happened so fast, she could hardly follow it all, yet Keegan had managed to react with preternatural speed, defusing a volatile situation in less than a minute. As she watched him walk toward her, his long-legged gait graceful but powerful, his big hands loose at his sides, she reflected that this was a man who truly knew how to handle himself. He had a brain to go with all that brawn—and guts. She couldn't recall ever having seen anyone—outside of TV and the movies—put himself on the line like that, risking his own safety for some greater purpose.

His fearlessness excited her, she realized with abashed amazement, thrilled her on a primal level—a *sexual* level—that she had never experienced before. *Instinct. The lure of the guy who kills the bears.* As he approached her, her heart began to pound in her chest, and she couldn't manage to tear her gaze from his.

"Well done," said Alden. "One more miscreant off the streets."

"'Fraid not," Jamie said. "By tonight he'll be out on bail and raising just as much hell as ever."

Alden shook his head disgustedly. "Figures. The Finns really know how to play the system. The only one I have any use for is Tommy. He's on my maintenance staff, and I must say, he's not a bad worker. I actually kind of like the kid."

"He's the best of them," Jamie agreed.

"Well, Jamie…" Alden shook the younger man's hand. "You're a handy man with a two-by-four. I've got a three o'clock meeting, or I'd buy you a beer."

"I couldn't drink it. I'm on duty."

"Ah. Of course. India, my dear, always a pleasure."

"Same here, Alden."

As the older man walked away, Keegan smiled wryly at India. "*Told* you Darrell was the worst of the lot."

She nodded and forced herself to look away from him, toward the crowd. Officer Billy wrestled Darrell into his patrol car while the Finns jeered—all except Tommy, who stood to the side with his arms wrapped protectively around Missy and the baby.

"Seeing Tommy like that," India said, shaking her head, "it's hard to believe he'd be capable of setting all those—"

She gasped as Phoenix jumped from her arms and tore out across the lot. To her surprise, he headed directly for Tommy, rising up on his hind legs to paw the young man beseechingly.

"Phoenix!" India crossed the tape and pulled the big tom back into her arms. As soon as she touched him, her mental TV switched on and a picture filled her mind—a picture of Tommy Finn opening a small can and placing it on the floor. She felt Phoenix's excitement, his eager anticipation as he sniffed at the contents of the open can.

Tuna! She smelled tuna! Phoenix's love of it was obviously so intense that even the memory of it conjured up its scent in his mind . . . and therefore India's. She had never actually *smelled* a psychic image before, and it left her feeling a little disoriented.

"Dr. Cook?" Keegan started to reach out to her and then stopped himself. "Are you . . ."

"I'm fine." She turned to Tommy Finn. "You know this cat, don't you?"

Tommy's eyes widened momentarily, then he swiftly marshaled his expression, throwing in a little sneer for good measure. "Lady, I never *seen* this cat till now."

"No?" He wouldn't meet her eyes, just looked around nervously, grinning and shaking his head. "I think you have. I think you've fed him tuna fish."

"Tuna fish?" He backed up, his arm around Missy, his gaze on the cat. "Uh-uh, lady. You got the wrong guy."

"I don't think so," she persisted as Tommy and Missy turned and began walking away. "I think—"

"Let them go," Keegan said.

"But—"

"But he's lying," he said quietly. "I know."

India gaped at him. "You do?"

"Absolutely." He grinned.

"It's that blue sense Sam was talking about, isn't it?"

"It's *common* sense. *You* saw the look on his face. You don't have to have ESP to know that guy was lying through his teeth. As to the part about the tuna . . ." He shrugged. "Seems a likely thing to feed a stray cat if you don't have any cat food in the house." He tapped his forehead. "Deductive reasoning."

"Ah. Then have you deduced *why* Tommy was lying?"

Jamie shielded his eyes to watch the young couple drive away in Tommy's battered T-bird, the baby in a car seat in back. "He doesn't want to associate himself with the cat. I suppose he knows there's some connection to the fire at Little Eddie's. That doesn't prove he's the Firefly, though."

"No," India murmured thoughtfully. "It doesn't."

Jamie's eyebrows rose. "Rescinding your accusation, Dr. Cook?"

"I never accused him," she pointed out. "He seemed the most likely candidate, but now . . . I don't know. Seeing him today . . ."

"Compared to Darrell, he doesn't look half-bad, does he?"

"No," she said candidly. "He doesn't. I don't know what to think."

Keegan let out a long, weary sigh. "That makes two of us, then."

5

HAVING NO APPOINTMENTS the next day, India spent the morning painting the dining room ceiling. She broke for lunch at one, then pulled on a pair of woolen gloves and walked down to the road to get her mail.

She always wore gloves when she went to the mailbox. Bills, magazines, and junk mail, being machine-processed, generally held no lingering psychometric energy, but human-produced mail did. It wasn't so bad if there was only one card or letter in the box; she could deal with a single correspondent's vibrations. But if there were two or more, the vibes tended to mingle, creating a jumbled psychic resonance, similar to when a radio was caught between two stations and picked up bits and pieces of two different broadcasts. The effect was maddening—just one more way in which her psychic "gifts" tormented her.

She sorted through the mail as she walked back up the gravel drive to the house . . . the phone bill, the latest issue of *Veterinary Economics*, and a plain white envelope. She turned the envelope over several times, feeling the weight of a letter inside, but finding no mark of any kind on the outside. No address, no postage, nothing. Obviously it had been hand-delivered.

She plucked a glove off with her teeth and held the envelope with her bare hand. Nothing. Standing completely still on the front porch of her house, she closed her eyes and concentrated. Still nothing. No vibes of any kind. Odd, considering someone had to have handled it at some point.

Stuffing the glove and the other mail under her arm, India tore open the envelope and unfolded the sheet of paper within.

She drew in a sharp breath. The magazine, bill and glove slipped to the floor of the porch. On numb legs, she walked to the kitchen, picked up the phone, and dialed information.

"What city, please?"

"Uh, Mansfield," she replied shakily. "The police department."

THE FRONT DOOR swung open as Jamie raised his fist to knock. The India Cook who greeted him—if you could call a blank stare a greeting—looked a far cry from her usual *Lady in Black*.

First of all, there were no sunglasses to hide those haunted coppery eyes, and her hair was mostly concealed beneath a neon yellow bandanna. She wore an oversize pink T-shirt—*sans* bra, he noted appreciatively—and blue leggings, heavily spattered with white paint. Her lack of footwear amused him primarily because of the revelation that her toenails were painted candy apple red. What kind of woman kept her fingernails short and bare, and painted her toenails red?

He raised his gaze to her face, finding it slightly flushed. "I didn't think I'd be seeing anyone today," she said self-consciously, turning and leading him through the foyer and across the hall. "It's in here."

Jamie heard the strain in her voice, and knew her nerves were stretched taut. He'd told her repeatedly on the phone to relax, to stay calm, that there was no real danger. Clearly his reassurances hadn't worked, and why should they have? So far, all he'd done was drag her, against her will, into danger's path. Not a sterling record on which to base promises of protection.

He followed her into a sizable living room, which, like the bedroom above it, was done up in warm off-whites, and featured a massive stone hearth. "There it is," she said, pointing to a sheet of paper lying atop a big marble coffee table.

While she paced the length of the room, Jamie set the briefcase housing his document evidence kit on the floor, hiked his trousers, and squatted next to the table. Like the Firefly's other notes, this one was comprised of mismatched cut-and-paste letters. But unlike his past messages, there was no mention of fire—only of death: "Back off, Witch. Or you'll wake up some morning with a bullet for a third eye. The Firefly."

Jamie placed the document kit on the table and unlatched it. He'd run the note into the lab, and then come back and check the mailbox and the surrounding road for further evidence—although if he had to wager a guess, he'd say it was unlikely he'd come up with anything. With one notable exception—the bit of burned magazine he'd found at the lumberyard—the Firefly seemed to know how to cover his tracks. Arson cases were always challenging, but this one was turning into a real nightmare, a nightmare with his captaincy hanging in the balance.

She stood over him, hands on hips. "You don't need to go to all that trouble," she said as he withdrew a pair of tweezers and used them to slide the note into a sheet protector. "They won't find any prints on that."

"Probably not, but you never know." He secured the evidence in the briefcase, relatched it, and rose.

"I *do* know," she said. "Whoever prepared that note wore heavy gloves. Not the thin latex kind he used with the other notes, but—"

"Whoa! Back up. How do you know about the latex gloves? Did Sam tell you?"

"No, Lieutenant, Sam didn't tell me." She stalked over to one of the bay windows flanking the fireplace and stared out at the rolling backyard. The afternoon sun glowed through her big T-shirt, revealing a wonderfully narrow waist and rounded hips. "Heavy gloves tend to muffle psi transmission, both on the sending and receiving ends. In other words, if someone wears them when he handles an object, the object is unlikely to absorb and retain his psychic energy. Likewise, if I'm wearing them when I touch something, I won't pick up other people's vibes. That's why you see me wearing gloves a lot."

"Uh-huh." His gaze strayed to her thighs and calves, firm and shapely beneath those skintight leggings. He hadn't realized what a fantastic body she had, and he almost wished he'd been kept in ignorance. She'd already gotten under his skin a lot more than was smart. He took a deep breath. "But how'd you figure out about the latex . . ."

She turned, unconsciously treating him to a brief and tantalizing silhouette of surprisingly generous breasts. "From what I gather, no fingerprints were found on the four arson notes."

He took a deep breath, trying to keep his mind on business. "That's right."

She came to face him across the coffee table. "But when I handled the fourth note, I got a reading off of it. Meaning whoever pasted the letters down on those notes found a method for keeping his fingerprints off the paper—but it's a method which doesn't prevent psi transmission.

Latex gloves are the obvious answer. They're very thin, and I've always been able to pick up psychic vibes through them."

Jamie was grudgingly impressed. She'd internalized this psychic delusion to the point where she could actually draw logical conclusions from it. Scary.

She cocked her head. "So how did *you* figure out he wore latex gloves?"

He chuckled. "The documents lab found traces of a powdered lubricant on the notes. It's the same kind of lubricant latex gloves are coated with."

"The wonders of modern criminology," she said dryly. "Too bad psychological profiles aren't as accurate as lab tests. You told me pyromaniacs don't go in for assault and murder. But now this particular pyro has gone and threatened to put a bullet in my brain some night while I'm sleeping."

"An idle threat," Jamie said in a tone he hoped sounded convincing. "I doubt he means to follow through."

She seemed to perk up, but then Jamie realized what was coming. "Oh, you *doubt* this madman means to sneak into my house some night and put a gun to my forehead and pull the trigger! Well, how comforting!"

He circled the table; she backed up. "Dr. Cook—"

Her eyes ignited. "You can't imagine how reassured I am to know there's only a *chance* I'll get my brains blown out in my sleep! What a relief!"

He held his hands up, palms out, and spoke in measured tones. "I'll take you off the case immediately. I'll announce it on the radio. I'll put it in the *Courier*."

She planted her hands on her hips. "Can you guarantee me—I mean a one hundred percent guarantee—that this raving lunatic won't try to follow through on this threat anyway?"

There was no use feeding a line of bull to a woman this smart. "No."

She nodded, looking very catlike in her anger. Jamie half expected to see claws pop out of the tips of her fingers. "So what am I supposed to do to protect myself?"

"I gave it a lot of thought on the way over. Is there any place you can go, relatives you can stay with until this all blows over—?"

"You've got to be kidding, Lieutenant." She was quivering. "I've got a veterinary practice to run, or hadn't you noticed? A brand-new practice at that, and none too solvent. Thank God I don't have a mortgage, or I'd never have lasted this long. If I leave town now, I'm going to lose what little business I've managed to drum up, and I can't afford that."

He rubbed his jaw. "I figured that might be a consideration."

"How can you be so damn blasé about all this?" she demanded furiously. "My life has been threatened, Lieutenant! There's a nut out there who wants to kill me, and if I run away from him, I lose my means of making a living. This is all your fault, Lieutenant. You realize that, don't you?"

"Absolutely."

"You did this to me. *You.*"

"I know."

"It's your responsibility, Lieutenant. If you hadn't—"

"Jamie."

"What?"

"I want you to call me Jamie."

She studied him, a stubborn set to her jaw. "I'd rather stick to Lieutenant, if you don't mind."

"I do mind. Call me Jamie."

She closed her eyes, as if straining for control. "Why?"

"Because then I'll get to call you India." She opened her eyes and blinked. He smiled and shrugged. "I've been wanting to call you India."

She blinked again, then looked away. From her wavering expression, he gathered she was trying to summon her rage back up, but having a hard time of it. Finally, with a weary sigh, she backed up and sank into the big overstuffed sofa, hugging a throw pillow to her chest. She looked sweet and lost and defenseless. "What am I going to do, Lieutenant?"

With exaggerated patience, he said, "You're going to call me Jamie." He knelt in front of her and looked into the troubled depths of her eyes. "And you're going to let me protect you." She looked toward the ceiling. "I know, I know. I got you into this mess. I've blown it, I admit it. That's why I want to make it right. I *need* to make it right. I can't just expose you to danger this way and walk away. But I can't tell *you* to walk away, either, if it'll destroy your practice."

"I'm waiting for some brilliant plan," she said listlessly.

He bit his lip, then came out with it. "The brilliant plan is that I stay with you." She just stared at him. "At night."

A pause. "Here?"

"Of course. Here in your house."

"Every night?"

"Until we apprehend the Firefly."

She looked thoughtful. "I've just moved here, and I've got my professional reputation.... What will people think?"

"They'll think we're sleeping together." He chuckled at her nonplussed expression. "Unless I spread it around that it's strictly police business, which I'll certainly want to do anyway, to warn the Firefly off."

"I'd have to fix up one of the empty bedrooms."

"No need. I won't be sleeping. I'll be pulling guard duty."

"Why you?" she asked. "You could order some patrolman to do it."

He stood. "First of all, I trust myself more than I trust even the best patrolman. Second, I'm the one who got you into this mess. I figure I should be the one to lose sleep over it."

"When *will* you sleep?"

"I'll leave work early and catch some shut-eye in the afternoons. During the day, I'll have a car watching the house. Then I'll be here from about eight o'clock till I go to work in the morning. So, what do you say?"

She looked off across the room for a few moments, seemingly lost in thought. Finally she said, "All right, Lieutenant. I really can't see any other way."

He crossed his arms as he looked down on her. "I'm going to call you India whether you call me Jamie or not. I can't spend the night with a woman I'm not on a first-name basis with."

Her mouth curved in a reluctant, lopsided smile, as if she were trying to fight it. "All right."

He grinned, sensing victory. "All right *what?*"

"All right, *Jamie*," she said with amused petulance.

"That's better." Grinning, he grabbed his document kit and headed for the door. "See you tonight."

INDIA CHECKED THE CLOCK when she turned on the shower that evening—6:35. She adjusted the stream to pulse and stood under it for a luxurious interlude, letting the hot jets of water pound some of the tension from her neck and shoulders. When she finally set about washing her hair and scrubbing off the paint, she felt far too mellow to rush the job. She dried herself off, slipped on white silk panties and a cropped, sleeveless T-shirt, and combed her hair in front of the full-length mirror on the back of her bedroom door.

The sound of footsteps made her drop the comb. She held her breath to listen, hearing a soft tread, and then another, and another, from the other side of the door. Someone was slowly climbing the stairs. Jamie? He wasn't due until eight o'clock; she hadn't even turned on the downstairs lights yet. And how would he have gotten into the house? All the doors were locked. How would *anyone* have gotten in? By breaking in—that's how.

With a shaking hand, she reached toward the doorknob, forgetting for a moment that there was no lock on it. Hissing a curse, she listened to the footsteps draw nearer.

A weapon! She ran on trembling legs to the mantel, opened a case at random, and pulled out a pistol—ancient and worthless, of course, but at least it *looked* kind of like the real thing. Then she slapped the wall switch, plunging the room into darkness, and positioned herself in the corner farthest from the door just as it flew open.

"I've got a gun!" she yelled as the dark figure materialized in the doorway.

There was a moment of silence, and then she heard a soft chuckle. "I've got *two*, and mine aren't flintlocks!"

She knew that voice. "Jamie?"

The lights went on, and she blinked. Jamie stood just inside the room, wearing jeans and a denim jacket, a gun held loosely at his side. The grin faded as his gaze swept over her thoroughly, taking in the short white T-shirt with its deep V neckline, and the satin bikini panties. His attention seemed to linger briefly on her bare stomach and legs, before he pulled himself together and cleared his throat. "Sorry. I didn't mean to scare you. Or, uh...you know...barge in on you." His ears, India noted, were bright pink.

India's legs felt wobbly, and she leaned back against the wall. "How'd you get in?"

"There was an unlocked window into your examining room. I'd rung the bell, but you didn't answer, and it was dark inside. I got worried." His gaze rested on her wet, combed-back hair. "You were in the shower, I guess."

Again his eyes seemed irresistibly drawn to her scantily clad body. India looked down at herself, suddenly very aware of all that bare skin. She automatically pulled her T-shirt down in a vain attempt to cover her midsection, only to find his attention suddenly riveted on her breasts as they pressed against the taut white cotton.

He backed up, gesturing toward the stairs with the gun. "I, uh...I'll be in the kitchen."

He shut the door behind him. India exhaled an unsteady breath, put the useless flintlock away, pulled on comfortingly sexless gray sweatpants and a matching sweatshirt, and went downstairs.

She found him at the kitchen table in front of an open box of fragrant pepperoni pizza, working on his second slice. "Want some?"

Grateful for his casual, everything-back-to-normal tone, she said, "Thanks. I'm starving."

She pried off a slice and sat opposite him. He'd taken off his denim jacket, and now wore a blue sweater, over which was strapped a shoulder holster. "Do you wear that thing all the time?" she asked.

"Only when I'm on duty. Does it bother you?"

"No." Actually, yes, but not in the way he meant. There was something unabashedly macho about the image he presented—a big, good-looking guy wolfing down pizza with a gun strapped to his chest. The gun shouldn't have intrigued her, shouldn't have increased his already potent sex appeal—yet it did. This had to be the height of political incorrectness, India thought ruefully, getting turned on by a gun! What was happening to her?

The men in her past had all been like Perry, urbane and coolly cerebral. They'd been the kind of men who liked to ponder things, discuss things, analyze things. James Keegan was the kind of man who took care of things. Plain and simple. He did what had to be done.

India finished her slice and reached for a new one just as Jamie did. As his hand neared hers, she flinched and drew back, sighing in relief that they hadn't touched. To cover her awkwardness, she rose and went to the fridge. "Soda? Water?"

"Water's fine."

She filled two glasses with ice water, handed him one, and sat down. He hadn't taken the slice he'd been reaching for, she noticed as she took a sip. It seemed he'd simply been watching her, his expression thoughtful.

"Can I ask you something, India? Something personal?" She nodded. "What happened to make you like this, so you can't stand being touched?"

"I assumed you knew," she said. "It's the psychic reception. Every time someone touches me, their thoughts just . . . fill me up." She shivered, and rubbed her arms. "I can't tell whose thoughts are whose. It makes me feel as if I'm losing my mind."

He nodded slowly. When he spoke, his words seemed chosen with great care. "I asked because, well . . . in my line of work, I've seen a lot of girls and women who've been victimized—abused, beaten, raped. Sometimes, especially if it happened when they were children, it leaves them very skittish about being touched."

So that's what this was all about. "That's not why I don't like to be touched, Jamie. I told you—it's my ESP."

He leaned forward on his elbows and spoke gently. "Are you sure? The human mind is very good at self-protection, India. It's not uncommon for someone who's been abused to block the experience from her memory—or to remember it as something other than what it was."

She gaped at him, dumbfounded. "You're serious. You think I've invented this whole psychic business to cover up—"

"Subconsciously, of course. I think it's a possibility. I know *something* happened to you when you were twelve. Alden told me it was a very traumatic time for you."

India laughed shortly. "'Traumatic'? You have absolutely no idea. Neither does Alden. You don't know what you're talking about, Jamie. Why don't you just drop this whole—"

"Because I like you." His gaze held hers solidly. "And I *don't* like the fact that you're terrified of the slightest touch from another human being. It's…it's horrible, it's crippling. How can you stand it?"

She swallowed hard. "I can't." She looked into his deep blue eyes, so full of misguided compassion, and added, "But I have no choice. That's the way it is."

He slapped a palm on the table. "Wrong. If something happened to you, you should face it. Try to remember. Go under hypnosis, if that's what it takes. You have to know the monster if you're going to fight it, India."

"Jamie, I *know* the monster!" She struggled to keep her voice steady. "*You're* the one who refuses to acknowledge it. Believe me, I remember every detail of what happened to me when I was twelve. And none of it involved abuse, sexual or otherwise."

"Are you sure? Have you ever explored the possibility? Maybe you should talk to somebody about it. Get professional—"

"You don't think I have?" She rose and pushed back her chair. "You're not the first person to decide I'm crazy, you know."

He stood also. "I don't think you're—"

"Save it." Her hands curled into fists; she quivered with frustration. "You know, I'm really sick of people like you, so full of good intentions, but so completely lacking in faith. I'm fed up with being doubted, fed up with having to prove myself . . . and I'm fed up with you!"

"India!" She swept past him and out the kitchen. He heard her take the stairs two at a time, and then came the muffled slam of her bedroom door.

With a groan, he sat down and dropped his head in his hands. *Nice goin', Keegan.* After a while, he put away the pizza, wiped the table down, and washed out the glasses. Then he checked and double-checked all the doors and windows, making a mental note to install proper locks tomorrow. When he was satisfied that the house was secure, he went upstairs and stood outside India's bedroom door for a full minute before summoning up the courage to knock.

Silence. Finally she said, "Please go away."

"I just want to apologize," he said.

Another pause. "Apology accepted."

"Face-to-face." He opened the door a crack. "India?"

She sighed. "Come in, then."

She reclined on her bed against a mountain of pillows, wearing those gray sweatpants and the sexy little

T-shirt he'd seen her in earlier, having tossed the sweatshirt onto the floor. The only light in the room came from the TV; one of her hands cradled the remote, while the other rested on Phoenix, curled up next to her. She looked heartbreakingly small and vulnerable.

As he crossed the room to her, she spared him a brief glance, then returned her attention to the TV, which she was watching with the sound off. She stared at the screen, soft blue lights shifting across her beautiful, tormented features. Jamie sat facing her on the bed, warily eyeing the cat on the other side of her.

He breathed in India's shower-fresh scent, warm and flowery, but not overly sweet. She pressed a button on the remote, and the blue lights began flickering to a different rhythm. After watching intently for a minute, she switched channels again.

Quietly Jamie said, "I can't seem to do anything right with you, India. Everything I say makes things worse. I hate that. I really do."

She let out a tremulous sigh. "It's just so frustrating to have this . . . this awesome power, this *thing* that totally controls my life, and know that I can't even talk about it, or people will think I'm nuts."

"You can talk about it to me," he said. "I guarantee you I won't think you're nuts."

"But you won't believe me."

After a moment's hesitation, he said, "I believe that whatever is happening to you is very real—to *you*. That doesn't mean you're of unsound mind. It just means you have stuff to deal with. I'd like to help you deal with it."

"Why?"

"I told you before—I like you. Just because I don't believe in psychic phenomena doesn't mean we have to be enemies. I'd like us to start over. I think we can find some common ground for friendship, but we have to trust each other. You have to trust *me*, even though I've been an ass. I know that's asking a lot."

She smiled crookedly. "Yes. It is."

He smiled, too, pleased at this little bit of progress. "Will you give me another chance, India? I just want to start off fresh. I want you to tell me about your powers, so I can understand what's happening to you."

"You won't try to get me to go to some shrink? Because I won't."

He nodded. "I understand. I won't try to pressure you into anything. I just want to hear about it. I want you to tell me what it's like for you."

She pointed to the TV. "That's what it's like, when I get visions." He turned and watched one image metamorphose into the next as she advanced the channels. "Except in black-and-white."

"You actually see pictures in your mind?"

"Yep." She stroked Phoenix from head to tail; he purred in luxurious satisfaction. *Ah, to be a cat.* Jamie watched her hand caress the gratified animal. "It's like I have an antenna inside me. In fact, I think the psychic energy I pick up on is actually a form of electrical energy—or something like it."

"And it started when you were twelve?"

"That's right. It's like the antenna began to activate, to pick up signals. I've read that the onset of psychic powers often coincides with puberty." She scratched the cat's throat; his eyes closed and he arched his head, giving her greater access. "The hormones or something."

"Did it come on all at once?"

"No, it kind of crept up on me, a little at a time. At first I just got vague feelings of distress when people touched me. Gradually it got worse and worse. In the beginning, my parents just thought I was—I don't know—making a play for attention or something. But when I told them I didn't want anyone to come near me, they took me to a shrink. By the time I was completely telepathic, I'd already been diagnosed as psychotically depressed. They didn't believe a word I said."

They didn't believe a word I said. He'd heard that before, from a young girl who'd lived through a nightmare of abuse, only to be told by those closest to her that she'd made it all up. So far, nothing India had said was inconsistent with his theory that she'd been somehow abused. What had really happened to trigger such a powerful delusion in her mind?

"Yeah, Alden told me your parents were skeptical."

A mirthless little laugh caught in her throat. "Skeptical? They thought I was insane. My father blamed my mother, and my mother blamed my father. She cracked first. About eight or nine months into the ordeal, she just packed her bags and took off."

"What did he do?"

"He had me committed."

"Oh, India." Unthinkingly, he started to reach for her, and she stiffened. "Sorry, I . . ."

"That's all right," she murmured.

"It must have been awful."

"It was," she confirmed. "It was two months of hell. You can't imagine."

"How'd you get out?"

"They gave me electroshock."

"Oh my God!"

"Yeah, that's what I thought when they started strapping me down for it. But you know what? It was the best thing that could have happened. When I woke up, the telepathy was gone."

"Just like that?"

"Just like that. That's one of the reasons I think psychic signals must be some form of electricity. Electrical currents seem to activate and deactivate the 'antenna.' The electroshock made my powers go away, and a bolt of lightning made them come back."

The logic she had invested in her psychic fantasy was impressive, but not foolproof. "Then what's to stop you from explaining all this to a psychiatrist and getting another shock treatment to make the problem go away?"

"I tried that," she said. "When I became psychic the second time, my ex-husband tried to have me committed again. I insisted all I needed was a dose of electroshock, but that was hopeless. None of the shrinks I talked to took my ESP story seriously. They looked up my past record and decided I was experiencing a recurrence of psychotic depression. If I hadn't divorced Perry, I have no doubt I'd be rotting away in some institution today."

She shrugged. "As it is, I've just had to learn to live with things the way they are. Actually, it's not the telepathy per se that bothers me so much. It's not being able to touch people. I can't hold a baby, shake hands, get a kiss on the cheek ..."

"Make love," he murmured.

She looked away and shook her head. They sat in charged silence for a few long moments. She rubbed Phoenix behind his ears; he growled with pleasure.

"Wait a minute," Jamie said. "You get psychic readings from animals, right? From cats?"

"Of course."

"Yet you've been sitting here petting Phoenix this whole time, with no problem. And you handle cats all day in your practice. How come you can touch them, and not people?"

"I couldn't, at first," she said, lightly running her hands over the cat's silken fur. "It drove me crazy. Really threw a wrench into my practice. Finally I had no choice but to force myself to handle them and deal with it as best I could. After a while, I realized I could consciously train myself to—I don't know—turn off the TV, if you will. Now it's really not a problem. For the most part, I don't pick up their thoughts at all, although every once in a while I still get ambushed, like when I first held Phoenix. Sometimes I deliberately tap in, like if I know a cat is in pain, but I don't know where it hurts."

"So when it comes to cats, you can turn your powers on and off at will," Jamie said excitedly. "Why couldn't you train yourself to do the same with people?"

She shook her head adamantly. "Impossible. The only reason I was able to do it with cats was because . . . well, because they *let* me. They had no choice. This didn't happen overnight, Jamie. It took time, and I had to handle a lot of cats before it got better. How would I possibly reproduce that process with people? Also, people's thoughts are more complex, more intense, than those of cats. I wouldn't really know how to go about it."

"How did you do it with cats? When you say you learned to 'turn off the TV,' what exactly does that mean?"

She shrugged. "I don't know . . ." She gazed with unfocused eyes at Phoenix. "I guess I kind of concentrate on . . . on being inside myself, if that makes any sense. I force myself to feel only what *I'm* feeling—the softness of the cat's fur against my skin, that kind of thing—and that seems to block the cat's thoughts from entering my mind. The more relaxed I am, the better it seems to work."

"That's just desensitization therapy," Jamie said confidently. "The substitution of relaxation for fear. A form of behavioral modification."

India's eyebrows shot up. "You sound like a shrink."

"I double-majored in psychology and criminal justice at Rutgers." He chuckled at her look of surprise. "You thought I was just some Irish cop from central casting."

"No. No, I—"

"Got a couple of master's degrees, too. Impressed?"

"Yes."

"Don't be. I just got them to help me make captain. Although I did learn a thing or two along the way. I think I learned enough to help you overcome this fear of being touched. Seeing as how you refuse to go for therapy, maybe we ought to give it a shot."

She stared at him. "I don't understand."

"I want to work with you," he said. "You and I may disagree about what made you so fearful of being touched, but we both know that's your primary problem. What I propose is that you let me help you solve that problem. We won't even talk about how you got this way. We'll just work with the symptoms, and if we're successful, maybe the underlying problem—whatever it is—will be easier to deal with."

"I don't know, Jamie. I don't think you understand what's involved."

"Touching." He smiled. "I have no real problem with letting you touch me."

Suspicion flared in her eyes. "Uh-huh..."

"No," he said shortly. "It's not what you're thinking. I know you don't know me real well, but I'm...I'm a nice guy. This isn't some elaborate scheme to get into your knickers, I promise."

She giggled. "Knickers?"

He grinned self-consciously. "Although, from what I saw, you've got lovely taste in them. I'm partial to silk."

"Is this kind of talk supposed to reassure me of your honorable intentions?"

"I'm not going to lie and say you're not an attractive woman, and if things were different . . . But they're not. You've got a problem, and I'd be a real rotter to take advantage of you."

She laughed again. "Rotter?"

"I probably shouldn't say this, but when you laugh, you just . . . you light up from inside. It's a beautiful thing to see. I wish you laughed more often."

She sobered. "There's not a lot to laugh about in my life."

"Then let me help. Let me make up for being such an ass."

She seemed to think it over. "What would be involved?"

"I think the thing to do would be to apply what you learned with the cats to people—to me. You just concentrate on what *you're* feeling, just as you did with the cats. We'll start very gradually, maybe just touching fingertips."

She bit her lip. "I can't do that. You don't understand. You don't know what it's like. The energy, it's so strong . . ."

"India—"

"It's not going to work, Jamie. People aren't like cats."

"India, just try—"

"No. I'm sorry, Jamie. I know you're just trying to help, but—"

"What if we didn't actually touch each other at first? What if we just touched the same object? Maybe that would filter the energy enough so you could handle it."

"Psychic energy generally doesn't pass through an inanimate object that way," she said.

He looked at her hand curled over Phoenix's back. "What about an *animate* object? Would that work?"

"Yeah, probably, but . . ." She noticed the direction of his gaze, and her mouth fell open. "You mean Phoenix?" He nodded. "You'd actually be willing to touch him? You're afraid of cats. I mean, you don't like—"

"No, I'm afraid of them," he confessed miserably.

"Why?"

"I have no idea. It's just a phobia I've always had." A bad one. He'd rather stick pins in his eyes than touch a cat.

"Forget it, then," she said. "It was a good idea, but—"

"No," he said, steeling himself. "I'll do it."

She blinked. "You don't have to. Trust me, I know about phobias. I've got one about fire. It'd be asking too much to expect you to—"

"I said I'll do it." His stomach tightened, and his heart began to beat erratically.

"Jamie—"

He held his breath and reached across her, his hand poised above the cat. Through an effort of will he kept it from trembling—*too* much. *It's just overactivity of the autonomic nervous system. You can control it.*

She lifted her hand from the cat. "I can't put you through this. Forget it, Jamie."

"I can take it if you can."

"Look at you," she said. "You're sweating. Let's not do this."

Slowly he lowered his hand, pausing when he felt the fur tickle his palm. His stomach clenched, and he inhaled deeply, commanding his muscles to relax. "Come on. I dare you."

6

INDIA SWALLOWED HARD, still unsure. She glanced toward Jamie, his gaze intent, his face pale in the dancing half light from the silent television.

He smiled; it looked forced. "If I can do it, you can." An anxious strain in his voice belied the bravado of his words.

India took a deep breath and extended her hand over Phoenix's head.

"Just feel what *you're* feeling," Jamie said softly. "Nothing more. And try to relax. You said that helps."

She closed her eyes and slowly lowered her hand until she felt the first soft suggestion of fur against her palm...and something else. A vibration, a kind of hum. At first she thought it was Phoenix purring, but then she realized this was different, like the muffled drone from a power line.

This had nothing to do with Phoenix. This was Jamie's energy. He *was* supercharged. Of all the people to try this with...!

"You can do it," he coaxed as she hesitated. "Rest your hand on him. Feel his fur. Just that."

She frowned, her eyes still tightly shut, and closed her hand gently over the back of Phoenix's head. Summoning all her mental strength, she tried to concentrate on the purely tactile pleasure of warm fur beneath her hand—but she couldn't. The droning was still there, making her palm tingle. It thrummed up her arm and spread throughout her body, which tensed in response. Her stomach lurched, her heart raced.

Fear.

Her eyes flew open, but still the harrowing picture lingered in her mind—the grainy black-and-white image of a cat, teeth bared, claws unsheathed, snarling. A jolt of terror seized her. Gasping, she drew back and wrapped her arms around her updrawn knees. The startled cat leapt from the bed and dashed across the room, disappearing through the open door.

Jamie moved closer, but didn't touch her. "India? What happened?"

"Th-the cat," she managed. "You *are* afraid. *Really* afraid."

After a moment, he nodded. "Was it that obvious how bad it was? I thought I was being pretty cool."

"You were," she said, impressed. "But I could tell. Why did you put yourself through that?"

He shrugged. "It was the only way to get you to try. I had to make you try."

His selflessness moved her. "Thank you." She shrugged. "But I tried, and it didn't work. So that's the end of that."

His expression said, *Is that so?* "The only reason I suggested using Phoenix was to ease you into the idea of being touched. We don't have to use him if he just gets in the way. Let's try my original idea—just touching fingertips."

She ran a hand through her hair. "Jamie, it's not that I don't appreciate what you're doing. You handled Phoenix, and I know that took a lot. But this just isn't working."

"Because you weren't relaxed. Neither was I. We've both got to chill out."

"Jamie—"

"Lie down and close your eyes."

India laughed nervously. "Jamie, no. Look, why don't you just admit defeat and go downstairs and—"

"I'm not very good at admitting defeat. Lie down and—"

"Why?"

"I'm going to try some relaxation techniques on you."

She narrowed her eyes. "Stuff you learned in your psychology courses?"

"Yep."

"Forget it. I hate that kind of stuff. I hate shrinks and all their mumbo jumbo."

"I'm not a shrink. I'm not even pretending to be one. Just a friend trying to help you with a problem." She shook her head resolutely. "I'm not going downstairs till you do it."

"Well, then, it's going to be a long night, isn't it?"

"I guess so." Jamie untied his sneakers and yanked them off.

"What are you doing?"

"Getting comfortable." He reclined on his side next to her, resting his weight on one elbow.

"Get out of here!" She backed up, grabbed a pillow, and hurled it at him.

He saw it coming and caught it easily, then studied her for a moment. There was a glimmer of distress in her eyes, competing with the anger. "Are you afraid of me?"

She lifted her chin. "Of course not."

"I mean, I'd understand it if you were, given your background."

She groaned. "For the last time, I was not abused!"

"No? Then how come you're afraid of me?"

"I'm *not* afraid of you! I *told* you!"

"You just don't like me."

"No, I—" again she raked her fingers through her hair "—I guess I like you all right, I just—"

"You just don't trust me."

"I *do* trust you!"

He sat up. "If you like me, and you trust me, and you're not afraid of me, then prove it. Lie down and close your eyes." She stared at him, her thoughts unreadable. "I promise you," he added with a smile, "I'm not leaving this bed until you do."

She looked away from him for a long moment, and then grudgingly scooted down on the bed and stretched out, albeit rather stiffly. He picked up the pillow she'd thrown at him and fluffed it. "Lift your head." She did, and he tucked the pillow in place, noting a bit of white fluff peeking from a seam. He slid it out and found it to be a dainty little pinfeather, about an inch long.

"Do I *have* to close my eyes?" she asked.

He held the feather by its shaft, twirling it. "Yes. I want you completely relaxed, and I want your attention focused on what you're feeling, not what you're seeing."

She closed her eyes. "I don't feel anything."

"Sure you do." He moved closer and looked down on her, rigidly supine, her hands clenched at her sides. "You can feel the room around you, the bed underneath you."

"Yeah, well—"

"You can feel the clothes on your body. Cotton and fleece . . . and silk."

"Uh . . ."

"Shh." He touched the feather to her lips. "No talking." She flinched, her eyes opening wide. "It's just a feather," he said, showing it to her. "Close your eyes."

After a moment's hesitation, she did.

"Breathe in deeply and then let it out slowly." He saw her chest rise and fall as she complied. "And again...and again. Let go of your tension. Let your muscles relax. Let your body float."

He continued his soothing litany for some time, keeping his voice low. Finally he saw her hands partially unclench. *Ah. Progress.*

He brought the feather to his own mouth and swept it lightly across his lips, leaving a whispery trail of sensation. Smiling to himself, he reached down and did the same to India. Her lips parted slightly.

"Just feel the feather, and nothing else." He trailed the downy tuft in slow paths over her face...along her nose, up the delicate line of her jaw, and over a finely carved cheekbone. Her skin was flawless, like white marble, and so translucent that he could make out a lacy network of violet veins beneath each eyelid as he stroked them with the feather. God, even with those amazing eyes closed, she was beautiful. Phenomenally beautiful.

"Don't think about anything," he murmured. "Just feel." He stroked the feather around the rosy edge of one ear and down her throat.

With languorous detachment he watched his hand guide the feather in circles over the exposed skin of her chest, then slowly trace the low V neck of her T-shirt. She didn't move a muscle, but he saw her nipples stiffen beneath the crisp white cotton. Arousal flashed through him. He froze, stunned that such a simple thing should affect him so intensely. *Easy, Keegan. You told her you were a nice guy.*

Her eyelids fluttered open. "What . . ."

"Shh . . ." He touched the feather once to each eyelid. She sighed and closed her eyes.

He took a deep, steadying breath, then reached across her, drawing the feather down the silken underside of her left arm from shoulder to wrist, and then up again. Her breathing quickened; his followed suit. Was there *no* part of this woman's body that wasn't an erogenous zone?

India was in a state of dreamy shock. For the most part, no one had touched her—other than to bump into her or brush against her—in years. And no one had *ever* touched her like this. Granted, it wasn't a human touch; it wasn't skin against skin. But it was the next best thing, tender and sensual, soothing and thrilling. If James Keegan could do all this with a feather, she wondered, what could he do with his hands, his mouth...?

She felt the airy brush of the feather against her palm, and sighed, her fingers opening of their own accord.

"Just feel," Jamie whispered.

"Mmm." She didn't have to be told. He'd mesmerized her, reduced her to pure feeling, pure pleasure.

The feather caressed her fingers, up and down, from the tips to the palm and back again. Gradually the caress intensified, leaving trails of ticklish warmth in its wake. A kind of rough smoothness replaced the insubstantial softness of the feather, and she felt not one point of sensation, but two, then three, then four...

"Oh, my God," she breathed when she realized he'd substituted his fingertips for the feather!

"Just feel," Jamie implored.

"Oh, my God."

She lay perfectly still, suspended in a realm of unreality, feeling nothing but the warm, electric touch of his fingers—his flesh against hers!—and the riotous pounding of her heart.

Just feel just feel just feel... she chanted inwardly, reveling in the moment, this magic, delicious, spellbound moment. He was touching her, and that was all she felt—his heat, the pleasing roughness of his callused fingertips...no jittery TV images, no alien thoughts and feelings.

"This can't be," she whispered as hot tears slid from the outer corners of her closed eyes.

"Sure it can." She sensed movement and opened her eyes to find him reaching toward her face. She stiffened automatically as his fingers brushed the tears from her cheek.

"No!" she gasped. She rolled away from him, but it was too late. Her mind exploded with shifting images— her eyes, her tears, her fingers, her breasts... She felt his desire, his confusion, but most of all his compassion, before the unwanted feelings subsided, leaving her breathless.

"Are you all right?" he asked. "What went wrong?"

She sat up, cross-legged. "It was when you touched my face. I wasn't expecting it. It . . . kind of broke the spell, I guess."

He plucked a tissue from the box on her night table and handed it to her. "A spell? Is that what it was like?"

She nodded, wiping her face. "It was . . . magical. But tenuous. Fragile. I kept worrying it would end." She let out a giant breath and shook her head. "I can't believe it. I can't believe it really happened. You touched me— you actually touched me, with your hand."

"For about three or four seconds."

"Is that all it was? It felt longer. It was...extraordinary. The most extraordinary thing that's happened to me, well, since the lightning." She laughed as fresh tears filled her eyes. "I can't believe it! You touched me! And that's all I felt. No vibes, no thoughts, no pictures. I didn't think it was possible."

Jamie grinned broadly, looking very pleased with himself. "Never underestimate the power of a feather." He rose from the bed and stood over her, the bit of delicate white fluff poised in the palm on his hand. He still wore the shoulder holster, from which the blue steel grip of his gun emerged. India was struck by the incongruous image of this big, burly, well-armed guy contemplating a feather—the feather he had wielded with such patient and sensual skill. He'd used that skill to coax her into a state of physical awareness so intense that she'd actually been able, for the first time in four years, to be touched by another human being without reading his thoughts.

No, Detective Lieutenant James Keegan was anything but an Irish cop from central casting. He was an enigma, a man who could face down a raving, stiletto-wielding crack-head, but was scared to death of cats. A man who was strong, passionate, sexy... and achingly tender.

Careful, India... You could end up really falling for this guy.

"Tomorrow night we'll do it again." Jamie lifted his palm to his mouth and blew on the little feather, which drifted toward India. She reached out and caught it in her hand.

"Only," he added as he turned toward the door, "without the feather."

JAMIE STOOD in the predawn darkness outside India's bedroom door, wondering if he should knock. If she was still sleeping, he didn't want to wake her. But if she was awake, he didn't want to catch her in her underwear again. Correction: *shouldn't* catch her in her underwear again. What he wanted was a different matter entirely, and something he'd better try to keep a lid on.

Finally he eased the door open and stepped inside. A faint hint of dawn glowed through the curtains, barely illuminating the room. Jamie came to stand over the big bed and the woman who lay soundly asleep beneath the white comforter.

Or mostly beneath it. It had been tossed back, leaving her uncovered from the waist up. She lay faceup, her head tilted in his direction, a swath of inky hair obscuring her face. Her nightgown was a gleaming little slip of champagne-colored satin with spaghetti straps. One of the straps had slid off her shoulder, exposing the creamy upper slope of a breast, and giving her a sweetly wanton air.

He would never think of her as *The Lady in Black* again. Beneath the grim black outfits and the shades and the gloves, she was all silk and satin and crimson toenails, hinting at a profoundly sensual nature held in check. He remembered how she'd reacted, with tears of disbelieving joy, when he'd finally brushed his fingertips against hers. In truth, she was as needful of human touch as anyone else—more so, perhaps, since she'd denied it to herself for so long.

Fast asleep, with her hair and gown all mussed and her perfect lips half-open, she struck him as both vulnerable and incredibly sexy, arousing his protective instinct, and another, more primal urge. He wanted to brush her hair back off her face. He also wanted to straighten that unruly spaghetti strap—or perhaps to take hold of it, and the other, and draw them down....

He shook his head to dispel the image of India lying soft and warm and naked in the pale dawn semidarkness . . . India looking at him with her mysterious golden eyes, wrapping her arms around him, saying his name...and he did *not* move to straighten that strap. But he did reach out to gently smooth the wayward lock of hair off of her face. Her cheek was incredibly soft; her skin radiated heat.

She moaned softly and shifted, her arms moving slightly, as if embracing the air. Then she murmured something that sounded like "Jamie . . ."

Her eyes remained closed, and after a moment her breathing regained its steady rhythm. Was she dreaming about him? Was it possible that, when his fingers brushed her face, she sensed that it was he who touched her? Could she even have absorbed his thoughts, his fantasy of her taking him in her arms and saying his name . . . ?

No. She couldn't have. He must be more tired than he'd thought, after his long night of guard duty, to entertain such a notion. Shaking his head, he remembered why he'd come to her room in the first place—his sneakers. He scooped them off the floor next to her bed and crossed to the door. As he started to close it behind him, he heard his name again and paused, then looked back toward the bed.

She was sitting up, adjusting the strap of the gown. Her hair was all askew, and she blinked drowsily. Jamie didn't think he'd ever seen a prettier sight.

"Sorry to wake you." He held up the sneakers. "I came for these."

"Oh." She nodded and yawned, then stretched her arms, quivering like a cat. Through a profound effort of will, Jamie kept from dropping the sneakers.

"What time is it?" she asked.

He checked his watch. "Almost six-thirty. I've got to run back to my place to shower and change if I'm going to get to the station on time."

She ran her fingers through her hair, which only further disheveled it. "You could . . . I guess you could bring a change of clothes and shower here in the mornings. If it would save you time."

"Thanks. I'll take you up on that. Do you like Chinese?"

"Sorry?"

"Chinese food. Thought I'd bring some tonight. Szechuan okay with you?"

"Mmm . . ." She yawned again, arching her back and unconsciously thrusting her satin-clad breasts forward. "The hotter, the better."

Both sneakers fell to the floor with a *thump*. Jamie retrieved them and fumbled for the doorknob. "Good. Great. Go back to sleep. See you tonight."

"FORTUNE COOKIE?"

"Sure." India opened her palm. Jamie reached across the coffee table, littered with the remains of their meal, to drop the cookie in her hand. She snapped it open and slid out the little slip of paper.

"What does it say?" he asked, stacking empty take-out containers and gathering up chopsticks and packets of soy sauce.

India squinted to read her fortune, the only light in the living room coming from the fireplace: *"You have met your true love."*

"Well?" He dropped the trash into the brown paper bag from the Chinese restaurant and folded the top.

India popped the cookie into her mouth and thought fast while she chewed and swallowed it. "It says, 'Your dearest wish will come true.'" She enclosed the little paper in her fist, rose from the sofa, and walked over to the fireplace. Kneeling, she parted the screen and tossed the slip into the flames.

"Wait," he said as she started to close the screen. Squatting next to her on the thick rug, he pulled a folded sheet of paper from the back pocket of his jeans and handed it to her. "You can feed this to the fire, too."

India unfolded the paper, swearing under her breath when she saw what it was. "This week something big goes up" read the photocopied cut-and-paste message. "Get ready. The Firefly."

"When did this come?" she asked.

"This afternoon. Burn it. I don't even want to feel it in my pocket. I just want to forget about this whole case tonight and enjoy being with you."

Enjoy being with you... India liked the way that sounded, as if he had come here, not to stand guard over her, but for the simple pleasure of her company. Almost as if this were a date, and not police business.

India wadded the note into a ball and threw it into the fire. She watched the flames consume it, reliving in her mind the strange dream she'd awakened from this morning. She'd been looking down on herself in bed, seeing herself as a lover might see her, her eyes dreamily seductive, her embrace warm and irresistible. *Jamie*, she'd murmured, only to open her eyes and find him in her room.

After he'd left, sleep had reclaimed her, ambushing her with the most deeply erotic dream she'd ever had. She woke in a sweat, breathless, overwhelmed, and half convinced it had really happened—that Jamie had come to her, had taken her in his arms and claimed her with an almost savage intensity. She'd lain in bed for some time afterward, shaken and dazed. This was more than desire. This was *need*.

"So what *is* your dearest wish?" Jamie asked as she pulled the screen closed.

She blinked at him.

"Your fortune said your dearest wish would come true," he reminded her. "I wondered what that might be."

Firelight danced in his eyes—eyes that seemed to look right through her, into her heart and mind. How much did they see? Returning her gaze to the flames, she said, "I don't know. To be able to . . . be touched, I guess."

"We're working on that. We'll try it again tonight."

Without the feather . . . India cleared her throat. "What's *your* fortune?"

"I don't believe in that stuff, remember?" He stood, taking the brown bag in one hand and a pile of dishes in the other.

"I'm a terrible hostess. Let me help you with those things."

She started to rise, but he said, "I'm a bodyguard, not a guest. Relax."

He returned from the kitchen with two cups of black coffee, sat back down next to her on the rug, and handed her one. Cradling the hot mug in her hands, she said, "You don't believe in any of it? Any kind of paranormal phenomena?"

He shook his head and blew on his coffee. "I think people tend to be very gullible. Unfortunately, there are plenty of scam artists out there who are more than willing to take advantage of that gullibility for their own gain. And then there are those, like yourself, who truly believe themselves to be possessed of special powers, but . . ." He paused, clearly uneasy. "India, perhaps we'd best not talk about this."

"I can take it. I'm curious. How do you explain all the amazing revelations and predictions psychics come up with?"

He waved a dismissive hand. "Partly tricks, and partly deductive reasoning. A smart cold reader can play a mark—"

"Cold reader?"

Jamie hesitated, looking vaguely uncomfortable. He sipped his coffee pensively. "Cold reading is when a phony psychic sits down with someone he's never met before and tells him all about himself, to establish credibility. The good ones are eerily accurate—you'd be amazed. But it's really all highly refined deductive reasoning, plus, as I said, a few tricks of the trade."

"You seem to have made quite a study of the subject." She swallowed some coffee.

He wouldn't meet her eyes. "I knew someone once who did it for a living. She'd pick a mark, one with money, and set up a cold read. She was brilliant at it, too—really knew what she was doing." A cheerless little laugh. "By the end of the session, she'd be telling the poor son of a bitch the name of the cocker spaniel he had when he was three. She was very observant, very charismatic, and she had about a thousand clever little tricks up her sleeve. Once she'd established the guy's trust, she could milk him dry."

"How? They'd give her money?"

"Oh, yes. Quite a bit of money. Sometimes it was just fees for the readings, but she'd charge whatever the market could bear, and con the marks into coming to her two or three times a week. She'd give them advice, tell them how to invest their money, how to conduct their love lives.... They'd grow dependent on her to the point where they couldn't make a move without consulting her. She'd string a bunch of them along that way, but that wasn't enough for her. If there was a way to squeeze an extra buck out of a mark, she'd squeeze it. She sold love potions, healing potions, tarot readings, hypnosis sessions, astrological charts . . . even séances."

"Sounds as if you knew her pretty well."

He hesitated, then seemed to come to a decision. "She was my aunt. Her name was Bridey. I lived with her."

Surprise flickered across India's features. "In Ireland, or . . ."

He shook his head. "My parents died in an auto accident when I was ten. That's when I came to Brooklyn and lived with Aunt Bridey."

"I'm sorry about your parents. It must have been an interesting experience, though, living with a . . ."

"Con artist," he said clearly, then added grimly, "Yeah, I guess you could call it interesting."

India nodded slowly. "So that's why you think all psychics are phony?"

He shrugged. "I grew up having it drummed into my head by Aunt Bridey that it was all a scam, that there was no such thing as true ESP. You just had to learn the tricks. One of them was using the police to help establish your credibility. Make it look like you'd solved a case—" he shrugged "—and the suckers would come running, waving fistfuls of cash."

"Jamie, I'm not denying that phony psychics exist, but that doesn't mean there's no such thing as ESP. You've got some yourself."

His brows drew together momentarily, and then he laughed. "My 'blue sense'? Don't believe everything Sam tells you, darlin'."

Darlin'. The word sounded very earthy, very Irish, coming from him. *Darlin'.* It felt like a big hand caressing her heart, leaving her weak and breathless. Ridiculous. He didn't mean anything by it. He called Sylvie the same thing, for heaven's sake. Still . . .

"I'm not psychic," Jamie insisted, "just a good detective. I'm observant, and I can put two and two together in my sleep. I see things I'm not even aware I'm seeing, hear things that don't register. Then suddenly all the pieces snap into place and I . . . *know* things. I get feelings about things. I try not to pay too much attention to them. I'd go crazy if I did."

"Sam's right, you *do* protest too much. You refuse to believe the obvious—that you have a little bit of psychic power. I'll tell you what's dangerous, Jamie. It's dangerous to have a power and not believe in it. Because if you fight it too hard, you'll end up ignoring things you should pay attention to. Like when you passed that 7-Eleven store and got the feeling something was wrong and stopped a robbery. What if you'd ignored that feeling and not gone in?"

Jamie sighed heavily and set his cup down on the coffee table, then took India's out of her hand and did the same with it. He grabbed a throw pillow and positioned it on the rug in front of the fire. "Put your head here and lie down."

She raised an eyebrow. "Are you always so authoritarian?"

"Only when I know what's best for someone. Now, lie down."

"Yes, Lieutenant." She lay on her back, smoothing down her big white T-shirt and crossing her legs, clad in black leggings. The rug, heated from the fireplace, felt delicious beneath her.

He lay on his side next to her, his head propped in his hand. "Close your eyes," he said quietly.

She looked up at him. He met her gaze with a look of reassurance. "It'll be okay."

She nodded and closed her eyes, taking a deep breath and letting it out slowly.

"That's good," he said. "Keep doing that. Clear your mind. Let your body float . . ."

Jamie's voice surrounded her, deep and soothing and unhurried. His words, underscored by the crackling of the fire, gradually drew the tension from her body, easing her little by little into a state of almost hypnotic relaxation. She lost all track of time. All she knew for sure was that she felt infinitely warm and weightless and tranquil.

"Feel the warmth . . ." he murmured. "It's so warm in front of the fire. The warmth surrounds you. It sinks into you. It becomes part of you, fills you up. . . ." She felt as if she were lying on hot sand beneath a blazing sun.

"Your skin feels hot . . . hot to the touch." A trail of sensation made its way slowly up her left arm, from wrist to elbow, then down again. India didn't move, although she felt her breath quicken. It was like being under the influence of nitrous oxide at the dentist's. You knew you were being drilled—you could feel it—but you didn't care. India knew she was being touched, but he'd brought her to such a state of altered consciousness that she could disassociate herself from that touch, could accept it, could *feel* it, without absorbing his thoughts.

"It's amazing," she whispered.

"Shh."

She felt it on her throat now, warm rivers of feeling as his fingers traced a path from her sternum to her chin, then up along her jaw on one side, and across one cheek.

A log popped loudly in the fireplace, and she started, groaning as she felt something reverse itself inside her, felt the TV in her mind flick on.

"No . . ."

"India—"

She swatted at him reflexively as the image of her own face snapped into focus for a moment, not black-and-white this time, but sepia-tinted with reflected firelight. Her eyes were closed, her mouth parted; she was exquisite.

"India, open your eyes," Jamie commanded as she covered her face with her hands.

The image began to dissolve. "Don't touch me!"

"I won't. Open your eyes. Come on." She took a deep, shaky breath and uncovered her face. Jamie was staring at her, his eyes filled with concern. "You okay?"

She nodded and sat up. "Yeah. It just kind of threw me, hearing that log pop. Sorry."

"It's not your fault, darlin'." India laughed wearily and shook her head. "What is it?" Jamie asked.

She bit her lip. "When you call me that, I feel like Sylvie."

His eyebrows rose. "Ah. Well. There are darlin's, and then there are darlin's."

"Which kind am I?"

He chuckled. "Persistent wench. You're the second kind."

"The second kind? What kind is that?"

He held her gaze. "I think you know." Warmth suffused her face; she looked away. Quietly he said, "I'm not planning on doing anything about it, you know." India felt both disappointed and relieved at this news. "I want you to feel safe with me," he said.

"I do."

His eyes glinted devilishly. "You wouldn't if you knew what I was thinking half the time."

India arched her eyebrows. "But I do. Funny thing is, I still feel safe with you." She shrugged and smiled. "Go figure."

7

THE PHONE RANG, jarring India out of her sleep. She opened her eyes in the dark and twisted her head around to read the clock. It was 2:49 in the morning. Groping around on the night table, she located the receiver and brought it to her ear. She opened her mouth to say "Hello," biting back the greeting when she heard a growled "Damn!"

That was Jamie's voice; he must have picked up the call downstairs. "When?" he asked.

"About ten minutes ago," another voice said. Deep and gravelly, with a pronounced drawl. Sam Garrett.

India replaced the receiver in its cradle, turned on a beside lamp, and belted her turquoise silk kimono over her nightgown. She finger-combed her hair as she padded downstairs in bare feet, mentally counting the number of days since the Firefly's fifth note had been received. That had been the day they'd had Chinese food—last Thursday—and it was Wednesday now. Correction: Thursday morning. The arsonist had waited a whole week this time before following through on his malicious promise.

During that week, patrol cars had guarded the house every day, and Jamie had stayed every night, reading and doing paperwork downstairs while she slept. Their evenings always followed the same pattern: a meal, some conversation, and then another session of experimental touching.

Progress had been made. Every evening Jamie got a little further—pushed the envelope a little more—before something triggered India's psychic reflex, shattering the enchantment. It now took only a minute or so before she was relaxed enough to be touched, and she didn't have to lie down, or even close her eyes. He had touched her arms, face, and throat—even rubbed her feet! To India, this was the most wonderful thing that had ever happened to her. Jamie seemed delighted by her progress, although sometimes she sensed strong desires kept under tight rein, especially when the "spell" broke and she absorbed his thoughts.

She found him in the brightly lit kitchen, gripping the phone under his chin while he penciled something on a scratch pad. "Yeah, Sam . . ." When he saw her, his eyes sparked with pleasure, despite the circumstances. Then he noticed her attire. His gaze raked her from head to toe, lingering for a moment on her chest, where the kimono gapped to reveal the lace bodice of her purple nightgown. "What? Yeah, I'll be there as soon as I'm relieved. Right."

He hung up the phone and slumped back against the kitchen counter, looking drained. "You know the Elm Plaza shopping strip on Jefferson and Elm?"

"Oh, no. The whole thing?"

"One end of it." He rubbed a hand over his jaw, dark with stubble. "They're fighting it now. We'll see what's left when the smoke clears."

"Do you have to go?"

He nodded. "ASAP. It's my case, after all. I'm meeting the state fire inspector there. Sam is sending a patrolman over to relieve me here."

"Go ahead, then. Leave now. I'll be fine."

With a tired smile, he shook his head. "No way. Not till my replacement gets here." He reached out to tuck a lock of hair behind her ear. His fingers brushed her cheek. "Oh—sorry..."

India waited for the TV to snap on, waited for his thoughts and feelings to bombard her. When they didn't, her mouth dropped open. Her hand went to her cheek, to the place he had touched. "Jamie..." She gaped at him, incredulous. This wasn't one of their carefully planned sessions, this was the real thing—an actual, spontaneous human touch, with no unwanted psychic transmissions!

Jamie grinned. "Yeah?" He tentatively reached out again. This time she held her breath. His fingertips trailed lightly down her face, from forehead to chin. All she felt was the warmth of his touch, nothing else.

Her eyes stung with impending tears, and she closed them. She felt his hands on her shoulders, through the silk of her robe. Then his arms encircled her, carefully, as if she were extremely breakable. "Is this okay?" he whispered hoarsely.

She could only nod as the tears overflowed. She reached around him and returned the embrace, astonished beyond measure to be able to do so.

He cupped the back of her head gingerly with his big hand and urged her to rest it on his chest. His rapid heartbeat thundered in her ear. "I can't believe it," she said in a broken voice.

"Believe it, darlin'." He threaded his fingers through her hair and rested his chin lightly on top of her head. He felt so large, so *warm*. She'd forgotten how warm people were, how their heat would seep into you, spreading throughout your body. She had fantasized so many times about what it would feel like to just hold another human being again. Now that it was actually happening, it seemed too good to be true.

She breathed in his subtle, masculine scent, reveled in the solidity of his broad chest through the thin cotton of his shirt. He held her closer and she molded herself to him, feeling the shape of his body, the hard edges of his gun and belt buckle.

The doorbell rang. "Easy," he urged as she stiffened at the interruption. "Just feel. Feel what *you* feel. Forget everything else."

That's easy for him to say. She struggled, her eyes squeezed shut, to turn off the powerful feelings—*his* powerful feeling—both of tenderness and longing. Hazy images scrolled through her mind, images of herself as he saw and felt her... her shapely body draped in supple silk, all soft and warm and vulnerable, pressed against him... her breasts crushed to his chest, her hips fitted to his...

"Feel what *you* feel," he gently commanded, without letting go of her.

The doorbell sounded again, but he ignored it.

"Turn it around, India. Turn off the TV. Pretend there's a remote control, and all you have to do is press a button."

Through a profound effort of will, she visualized a remote in her hand, and made her thumb depress the little red button.

The images blinked out. India gasped.

"Did it work?"

India nodded.

"It *did?*" he asked incredulously.

India laughed, rubbing at her tears. Jamie pulled a paper towel off the roll above the sink and gently blotted the wetness on her cheeks.

A rapping on the window startled them both. They turned to see a blond patrolman—India recognized him from the station—looking in on them from the patio. His expression of confusion transformed to sheepishness as he took in the loose embrace, the tears, and India's state of dishabille.

Jamie let the young officer in though the back door and introduced him as Len. After a brief battery of instructions to his replacement, he left for Elm Plaza, and India returned to her room. She lay in bed for some time, reliving the joy she'd felt when he took her in his arms and held her. It was as if he'd pushed open the dark, suffocating curtain that had enveloped her for so long. It was nothing short of a miracle.

FOR THE SECOND TIME that morning, India awoke to the ringing of the phone.

"Hello?" she muttered sleepily into the receiver.

She heard the receiver being lifted on the downstairs extension. "Hello," Len said.

"Ah, I've got you both." It was Jamie's voice. "Len, you can call it a night if you're so inclined. It's almost seven."

"Okay, Lieutenant."

A brief pause, then Jamie said, "Hang up the phone, Len."

"Oh. Okay. Bye, Lieutenant. Uh, bye, Dr. Cook." *Click.*

India sat up in bed. "How'd it go, Jamie? Any startling news?"

"I don't know if it's startling or not." He sounded very tired. "But I arrested Tommy Finn."

India envisioned Tommy Finn with his arms around Missy and the baby, and felt an empty sadness. "Oh."

A weary sigh. "Yeah, that's pretty much the way I feel about it. Christ, sometimes I hate this job."

"Why'd you arrest him?"

"I found his wallet in the Elm Plaza parking lot."

India mulled that over for a second. "His *wallet?*"

"Complete with driver's license, a photo of Missy, and $17.51," he said miserably. "How's that for incriminating evidence?"

"A little too incriminating, if you ask me," India said. "I mean, his *wallet?* What kind of a criminal drops his *wallet* at the scene of a crime?"

"A sloppy one."

India shook her head, even though he wasn't there to see. "The Firefly was never sloppy before. Why now? And a wallet, for God's sake. Just strikes me as bizarre."

"Trust me, that's not the strangest thing I've ever seen a perp leave behind. And it's also not our only physical evidence against him. I found something very interesting in his house when I arrested him." A pause; another enervated sigh. "But Sam seems to agree with you. He said it strikes him as a tad obvious. He wants you to come down and give the wallet the old psychic read. Would you mind?"

India replayed the carefully worded request in her mind. It was Sam, not Jamie, who wanted her to come to the station and check out the wallet. Despite Jamie's obvious affection for her, he was as skeptical of her powers as ever. This rationale he'd concocted to help him deal with it—that her ESP was really her mind's way of shielding her from repressed abuse—provided the perfect framework of logic for his disbelief. She tried to tell herself that it didn't matter, that they had enough of a rapport in other ways to make up for this lack of faith.

Only it did matter. Faith was faith. Either he believed her or he didn't. And he didn't. It really didn't matter why. India had had enough of being doubted. The people she'd been closest to—first her parents, and then her husband—had very nearly destroyed her with their doubt. She had promised herself when she left Perry that she'd never let that happen again. She'd never let herself get close to anyone who didn't believe in her powers. Yet she now found herself falling for a man who would never, "while there's a sun in the sky and fish in the sea," *ever* accept them. Could she break her promise to herself and have a relationship with someone who refused to accept her for what she was? *Should* she?

"India? Will you come?"

"What? Of course. I'll be there within the hour."

INDIA IDENTIFIED HERSELF to the woman officer at the front desk, who promptly escorted her through the station and into a small, darkened room. She'd expected Jamie, but found Sam instead. He greeted her warmly. "I like that sweater, kiddo. Red suits you."

"You think so?" She knew so. With her jet hair and pale skin, it was the perfect color for her, but this was the first time she'd worn it in four years.

Sam nodded toward a window leading into another room.

The other room was pleasantly furnished and much more brightly lit. Jamie sat in a large, executive style chair at one end of a small conference table, in the middle of which was a stack of magazines and his little tape recorder. He looked very commanding despite his sooty jeans and sweatshirt, and the dark circles under his eyes. She noticed he'd removed his shoulder holster. At the other end of the table, slumped in a smaller chair, sat

Tommy Finn, in identical attire, except cleaner. Both men could have made good use of a comb that morning.

When Jamie spoke, his words were audible in the room occupied by India and Sam through a microphone: "How long were you feeding the cat?"

India moved closer to the window, which she now realized was a two-way mirror.

Tommy shrugged, his dark eyes darting around nervously. "Couple of months."

Jamie wrote in his blue notebook. "Where'd you find him?"

"He used to hang around the house. Always sleeping in everybody's cars."

India turned to Sam and whispered, "Doesn't he have to have his lawyer with him?"

Sam shook his head and came to stand next to her. "He waived his right to counsel. Says he's innocent."

Jamie looked up from his notebook. "Did you ever take the cat to work with you?"

"To Lorillard?" Tommy folded his arms over his chest. "I didn't, like, *take* him. But half the time, he'd be stowed away in the back seat of my car when I got there."

"And you'd bring him inside while you worked."

"Sure. Didn't bother nobody. There was mice in the basement. He got off on trying to catch 'em."

India saw Jamie's jaw muscles clench, as if he were steeling himself. This must be hellish for him, she realized—playing the no-nonsense interrogator when, despite Tommy's presumed guilt, he felt something for the kid. "Did he stow away like that when you went to set fire to Little Eddie's?"

Tommy sneered and shook his head. "Nice try, man, but you got the wrong guy. I never set fire to no roadhouse. Or no lumberyard, neither."

"Or no strip mall?"

"Hell, no."

"Then how come your wallet ended up in the Elm Plaza parking lot?"

Tommy grimaced. "Wish I knew, man. It disappeared yesterday, but I thought it was just one of them things."

Jamie cocked an eyebrow. "That's very philosophical of you."

Tommy looked as if he weren't sure whether he'd been insulted or not. "Stuff turns up missing at home sometimes. There's all these kids around . . ." He shrugged elaborately.

Jamie rose, pulled out one of the smaller chairs, and sat close to Tommy, facing him squarely, his elbows resting on his knees. "Why'd you lie when Dr. Cook asked you about the cat at the lumberyard? You said you'd never fed him, never even seen him."

Tommy held his hands up. "Look, man, I wasn't under oath or nothin'. What's the big deal?"

"No big deal," Jamie said smoothly, "except you lied. I was just wondering why, that's all."

Tommy looked away, scrubbing his hands on his legs, and then met Jamie's direct gaze. "I just didn't want any trouble, is all. I heard they found Max at—"

"Max?"

"The cat. That's what I called him. I heard they found him at Little Eddie's after it burned down. Is that true?"

"Close enough," Jamie confirmed. He sat back and rested an ankle on the opposite knee. "So you didn't want to be connected with Max 'cause it might incriminate you."

"Somethin' like that. I can't get arrested, man. I can't be off the streets. That'd screw things up good."

"You *have* been arrested," Jamie reminded him.

"Yeah, well, I'm getting myself bailed out. I can't stay in here. I gotta get out today."

"What's the hurry?"

"That's my business."

Jamie's brows drew together. "You on dope, Tommy? You need a fix, is that it?"

"*Hell* no! I'm clean!"

Jamie nodded. "I thought so." Jamie regarded Tommy in silence for a moment. "Did you know we had your house under surveillance the night of the lumberyard fire?"

Tommy frowned at Jamie and recrossed his arms over his chest. "How come?"

"How come is my business," Jamie said. "Fact was, you never went home that night after your shift ended at Lorillard. Makes me wonder where you were while the lumberyard was being torched. Care to enlighten me?"

Tommy just stared at Jamie, obviously trying to make his expression as neutral as possible. But his eyes shifted nervously as he struggled to composed a response. Jamie crossed his own arms and sat back, regarding Tommy with studied patience. Tommy looked down at the table and rubbed his fingers over an invisible spot on the wood. His face took on a sheen of perspiration. India realized that Jamie was literally sweating him out.

Grinning, Sam turned to India and whispered, "I love watchin' Jamie interrogate folks. It's better than TV."

Finally Tommy said, "Man, I don't know what I'm doing here, answering this crap. A Finn can't get no justice in Mansfield. This town wishes we'd all drop dead. *I* know. I know what people think of us."

"Is that why you're burning the town down building by building?" Jamie asked. "To get back at Mansfield for—"

"No!" Tommy slammed a fist down on the table; the cords in his neck stood out. "I *told* you! I didn't do it!"

Jamie leaned forward until he was nose to nose with Tommy. "Then where were you the night the lumberyard burned up?"

Tommy pointedly looked away and drummed his fingers on the table. "This is bull," he muttered. "I don't have to answer this garbage."

"You do if you want an alibi."

"I didn't do it!" Tommy screamed. India sensed a kind of helpless frustration beneath his rage. *My God, he's telling the truth.*

"Oh, you did it, all right," Jamie said grimly.

"No," India whispered. From the corner of her eye, she saw Sam throw her a curious look.

"You don't know what you're talkin' about!" Tommy accused.

Jamie lifted the stack of magazines and held them in front of Tommy's face. "If you're so innocent, what were these doing under your bed when I arrested you this morning?"

"I never seen them before, but so what? They're just magazines."

Jamie tossed aside all but the top magazine—an issue of *Town & Country*—and opened it up to a page marked with a red tape flag, which he held up for Tommy's inspection. "They're just magazines in which letters from ads and headlines have been methodically cut out. I compared the missing letters to the latest arson note, and also to a note that was put in Dr. Cook's mailbox a week ago. They're an exact match. Do you have an explanation for that?"

"I told you I never seen them before," Tommy said angrily.

Jamie slapped the magazine down on the pile. "Just like you told us at the lumberyard that you never saw that cat before."

"This time I'm bein' straight with you," Tommy insisted.

Jamie leaned forward again, drilling his gaze into the younger man. "You want to be straight with me, Tommy? You want to save your sorry ass? Cooperate a little, for God's sake. Help me out." He seemed genuinely distraught; India sensed his frustration. "Give me an alibi to work with. Tell me where you were the night the lumberyard burned down."

Tommy shook his head forcefully. "Can't do that, man."

"Are you protecting someone?" Jamie asked.

Tommy sat up, alert. "What do you mean?"

India could see from Jamie's intent expression that he, too, had noted Tommy's sudden concern. "I mean is there someone else, an accomplice, maybe, who you're trying to cover for? Do you know who the Firefly is? Is he a friend of yours?"

Tommy relaxed, slumping down in his chair. "No, man, no. It's nothin' like that."

"What, then? Who else is involved? Who are you—"

"You know what, man? I think I *will* call my lawyer. 'Cause this is bogus. I don't think I should have to answer these questions."

A pause, and then Jamie shrugged with what India knew to be feigned indifference. "Suits me. I can use the break."

As Jamie led Tommy out of the interrogation room, Sam said, "So you think the kid's innocent, huh?"

India arched an eyebrow. "Does he look like the type who'd own a copy of *Town & Country*?" Sam greeted this observation with a sandy chuckle. "Yes," she said. "I think he's innocent."

"Come down to my office and see what kind of reading you get off the wallet. You can test your powers on those magazines, too. I'd be curious to see if that influences your opinion any."

JAMIE POURED THEIR COFFEE while India loaded the last of their dinner silverware into the dishwasher. Since Tommy Finn had, as promised, bailed himself out that afternoon, Jamie had no choice but to continue to guard India at night. Not that he minded. Although he hated that her life had been threatened, he relished spending this time with her.

It had been a remarkable week. His campaign to reacclimate her to human touch had become a journey of sensual discovery for them both. They'd grown to share a level of trust and affection he'd never experienced with a woman. All in all, for two people who'd started out on the wrong foot, they'd done surprisingly well together—until tonight.

They took their cups into the living room and sat next to each other on the couch, drinking their coffee in strained silence while they pretended to watch the flames cavort in the fireplace.

Finally Jamie said, "We've just got to agree to disagree about this, India. Although," he continued, attempting a casual tone, "it's kind of amusing that you and I have so completely reversed our positions on the subject of Tommy Finn."

"Amusing?" She turned to look at him, her amazing eyes pale gold in the flickering firelight. "This is a man's life we're talking about, Jamie."

A painful fact he knew all too well. "A man who's set five fires and threatened to kill you," he said pointedly.

"I *know* he didn't do those things," she said. "And if you'd just trust in your blue sense, you'd know it, too." He couldn't repress a smirk at that. "Admit it," she challenged. "Isn't it just a *little* convenient, finding his wallet at the scene of the crime?"

"I thought you told Sam you didn't get anyone's vibes off that wallet except Tommy's. Isn't that supposed to show that he was the only one who handled it?"

"Of course not," she countered. "The person who planted it wore heavy gloves, that's all. That's why I didn't get any readings at all off the magazines. By the time the Firefly cut the letters out of them for the death threat and the fifth arson note, he'd switched from latex gloves to heavy gloves."

"Why?"

She looked thoughtful. "Maybe he's figured out that's the only way to keep me from identifying him. At least *he* believes in my powers!"

"Speaking of those magazines," Jamie said, "do you have any clever rationalization for what they were doing under Tommy Finn's bed?"

"Oh, please." She reached to set her coffee cup on the table. The movement caused her oversize white shirt, the top three buttons of which were undone, to gap open momentarily. Jamie caught a brief flash of breast, including a rosy nipple, and just about dropped his cup in his lap. "If he *were* guilty," she said, "would he keep them, knowing how incriminating they were? He'd burn them, or at the very least, throw them away."

"So you think he's being framed."

She turned to face him, curling her blue-jeaned legs underneath her. "Seems the likeliest scenario."

"Who's doing the framing?"

"Someone who doesn't like him. Darrell, maybe."

Jamie snorted. "You think that crack-head's got it together enough to engineer something like this? I'm sorry, India, but the cold, hard fact of the matter is that Tommy Finn is guilty as hell. It doesn't matter what you and I want. The truth is the truth. It doesn't bow to sentiment, so I won't, either."

He drained his cup and set it down next to hers, then shook his head grimly. "Arresting Tommy Finn was one of the most painful things I've had to do in all my years on the force. No one wanted him to be innocent more than I did."

"You feel a kinship with him," she said quietly. "It's been obvious from the start. He reminds you of yourself at that age, doesn't he?"

He stared fixedly into the fire. "By the time I was his age, I was in college. But he does remind me of myself as a teenager. When I told you about Aunt Bridey, you said it must have been interesting living with her. You don't know the half of it."

"I'd like you to tell me."

He shook his head. "No one knows."

She moved closer to him. "I want to know. Jamie, look at me." He did. Her eyes were enormous in the firelight, warm bronze disks. "I trusted you when I let you touch me. Now I want you to trust me. Please."

"Oh, hell . . ." He rested his elbows on his knees and dropped his head in his hands. India was incapable of violating his trust; he knew that. And he had to tell her; he couldn't hold this back. But it would be easier if he didn't have to look at her. "Aunt Bridey was thrilled when I came to live with her. A child was the perfect prop for her scams. Usually she'd make me pretend to be her kid. She discovered she could extract more money from her suckers if she portrayed herself as a mother. Made her seem more respectable."

He glanced at India, who sat watching him closely, before continuing. "As I got older, I became an apprentice to her. Actually, I learned a lot from her that I still use today . . . body language, psychology, deductive reasoning. She taught me all her little tricks, and had me listen in on her readings so I'd learn how it was done. Now that she had a helper, her sessions got more elaborate. She put me in charge of special effects. I'd be the voices of the spirit guides, I'd rap on the walls, get the dry ice going, that sort of thing. The marks ate it up."

"You never felt, well . . ."

"I felt perfectly awful about it from time to time, when my conscience acted up. But you have to understand— Bridey was my surrogate mother. She was all I had. It never seriously occurred to me to refuse to help her. Until . . ."

He stared at the fire, losing himself in the flames. "There was this one . . . client. That's what she called them—clients. Mr. Hawley, Frank Hawley. He was about sixty, and loaded. His wife had just died, and he had no one. Except Bridey. The poor guy was so vulnerable, just an open wound, emotionally. She wanted him to disinherit his son and make her the beneficiary in his will. I told Bridey she was going too far this time, and I wouldn't help her. I didn't, but I just stood by while she worked on him. She did everything in her power to poison this man's relationship with his son."

"Did she succeed?" India asked softly.

"She did convince Mr. Hawley that his son hated him and was trying to have him declared incompetent and steal his estate. But she never did get written into his will.

He shot himself in the head before he had a chance to do that."

"He . . . oh, Jamie. Oh, how horrible."

"Yeah," he said bleakly. "I thought so. I was . . . consumed with guilt. I should have stopped her."

"What did you do?"

Jamie sat up and rotated his shoulders. "I told Aunt Bridey I was going to turn her in unless she quit the business. She moved back to Ireland, and I haven't heard from her since. I crashed with some older friends who had their own place until I was out of high school. Got a scholarship to Rutgers and discovered they taught criminal justice there. It was a refreshing change of pace."

She eyed him intently. "Is that why you became a detective? To atone for your youthful life of crime?"

He grinned. "Nah. Figured it'd be a good way to meet girls."

India laughed. "You're supposed to become a rock star if you want to meet girls."

"I don't know . . . I met *you*." Her right hand rested on the back of the sofa. He slowly covered it with his left, sighing in very real relief when her only response was a small smile of delight.

She shook her head fractionally. "I still can't believe it. Oh! I didn't tell you! This morning, when I handed the wallet back to Sam, I deliberately let our fingers touch." She grinned broadly. "I didn't feel anything. *Nothing*."

"Really?" He gently squeezed her hand. "I'm jealous of him. Isn't that idiotic? But I am. I hate the idea of your touching another man."

A shy look crossed her face, and she looked away for a moment, then returned her gaze to him. "But that was the whole point, right? You wanted to train me to be touched. And you succeeded. It worked. I don't know how to thank you."

Jamie had a few thoughts on the matter, but he kept them to himself. "You talk as if the process is finished."

She shook her head. "I have no illusions. It won't be finished for...maybe never. But thanks to you, I've reached a stage where I can function as a normal human being. I can survive having my fingers brush someone else's. I could probably bump up against someone without having a nervous breakdown. And I won't have to look for excuses not to shake hands anymore. That's enough for now."

"Is it?" he asked quietly, feeling suddenly shy himself, but overwhelmingly needful. "You wouldn't like to... take it further?"

She gazed at him for a long moment, and when she spoke, her words were so soft that he could barely hear them. "How much further?"

Gradually—very gradually, so she'd know it was coming—he leaned forward, bringing his face closer to hers by degrees as his free hand moved to encircle the back of her neck and guide her toward him. It all happened in dreamy slow motion. Her iridescent eyes locked with his. Jamie's heart pounded in anticipation; it hurt to breathe.

Her fingers tightened around his. He paused, his lips a hairbreadth from hers. "Darlin', if this doesn't feel right to you...I mean, I told you I wouldn't take advantage of you—"

She shook her head; their lips brushed. In an unsteady whisper, she said, "I don't feel like that's what's happening here."

She tilted her face up just enough for their lips to meet. Her eyes closed. Ecstatic that this was what she wanted, he kissed her, not too hard, cupping her head to hold her still as she released her grip on his hand and slid her arms around his neck. With his free hand he stroked her bare throat, feeling her pulse rioting just beneath the hot satin skin. He slid his fingers under the open collar of her shirt and along her delicate shoulder, issuing a mental warning to himself to take things slow. Too much aggression on his part could trigger unwanted memories, snapping deeply buried nightmares into sharp focus. He wanted to help her overcome whatever horrors she had been subjected to, not force her to relive them.

Despite his self-imposed restraint, he reveled in the kiss. Her lips were impossibly soft, deliciously warm; they tasted like coffee and lipstick. He inhaled that light, intoxicating perfume she wore. When he touched his tongue to the seam of her lips, they parted for him. He deepened the kiss experimentally, and she yielded with a tremulous sigh.

He was kissing India! This was what he'd wanted, what he'd needed, what he'd thought about constantly during the two weeks since that staged kiss at Lorillard Press. She was so hot and sweet, so achingly perfect. Caressing her throat, he drew back from the kiss and watched, breathless, as she slowly opened her eyes.

She smiled, her shimmering golden gaze holding his. "So, exactly how much further did you have in mind?"

Jamie returned her smile, then slowly lowered his hands to the buttons of her shirt.

8

INDIA WATCHED as he slid a button from its buttonhole. He paused, glancing at her as if to assure himself that this was okay, and then slipped a hand under the crisp white cotton. She felt his warm, callused fingertips graze the silky underside of her right breast, and went still, closing her eyes. That she could be touched this way, after thinking it would never happen again—to feel this heat, this intimacy, and nothing else—was almost more than she could accept.

Her heart raced in her chest. He kissed her again as he caressed her breasts with aching gentleness, lingering over the process as if all he wanted in the world was this. India felt her nipples tighten as his fingers brushed them. His featherlight touch was dizzyingly erotic.

He cradled her left breast in his big palm, his voice a rough whisper against her lips. "I can feel your heartbeat."

India lifted a hand and pressed it to his broad chest, feeling a rapid-fire thudding through the scratchy gray wool of his sweater. "I can feel yours, too."

Jamie caught her hand in his, shaking his head. "Just feel what *you* feel." He eased her down so that she lay against a mound of throw pillows. Sitting over her on the edge of the couch, he slowly finished unbuttoning her shirt.

He kissed her throat all over, and then parted her shirt slightly and kissed a path down the narrow strip of exposed flesh, and up again. She threaded her fingers through his hair as he pushed the shirt aside and lowered his mouth to her breasts. His kisses felt luxuriously sensual—hot and sweet and thrilling. When he took a stiff nipple between his lips and tugged, a jolt of sexual craving swept through India. She arched her back, needing more. "Jamie . . ."

His mouth closed over hers for another kiss, this one more demanding than the others, deeper, more urgent. Then he sat up. She heard the rip of Velcro as he swiftly removed his shoulder holster, withdrawing a big, boxy semiautomatic, which gleamed dully in the warm firelight. He tossed the holster aside and set the gun carefully on the coffee table. Clearly he meant to keep it within reach, a sobering reminder of his true function here. Bending over, he took off his sneakers, then raised a leg of his jeans and began fiddling with something around his ankle. India sat up and watched him remove a second holster, this one housing a snub-nosed revolver. "How many of those do you carry?"

He grinned at her over his shoulder as he pulled off his socks. "You want to search me for weapons, ma'am?"

His playful invitation took her by surprise. Lovemaking with Perry—and the few others before Perry—had always been rather grimly serious. But then, Jamie was so different from those others—thank God! After a moment's hesitation, she said, with a coy smile, "Do you think that's necessary?"

He shrugged. "Better safe than sorry." He rose and stood in front of the fireplace. "The light's better over here. I assume you want to be thorough."

She chuckled and came to stand before him, noting how his gaze was drawn to the inch-wide gap where her shirt was unbuttoned. "Let's see, now. Where might you conceal a weapon?" She made a show of inspecting his big body.

"I'll help you out." He grabbed the hem of his sweater and the T-shirt beneath, whipped them off together over his head, and tossed them onto the table.

India swallowed in very real astonishment as she took in the musculature of his massive torso and long arms. Her first thought was that *this* was how a man was supposed to look. Her second thought was that she had to touch him.

She did. With a shy glance at Jamie's face—his smile was more tender now than prankish—she stroked the breadth of his shoulders and ran her fingers through the dark hair of his chest. It felt surprisingly soft, the flesh beneath it a solid wall of muscle.

She wondered whether he had deliberately maneuvered her into a position wherein she, not he, would be the aggressor, and decided that he had. He probably thought she'd feel safer that way.

He held her gently by her shoulders and pressed his lips to the top of her head. She kissed his throat and chest, loving the taste of him, marveling at his size and strength and warmth. When he slipped her shirt down over her shoulders, she stepped back and let it fall to the floor. Firelight sparked in his eyes as he looked down on her, dressed, like him, in nothing but blue jeans. Then he drew her into his arms, holding her close, whispering her name, telling her she was beautiful.

She wrapped her arms around his waist, listening to his heart thunder in his chest. He leaned down and took her mouth again in a hungry kiss, his hands roaming over her, kneading and caressing. They slid down to the small of her back, pressing her toward him. She molded herself to him as his hands descended farther, closing over her bottom and crushing her hips to his. He moved against her in a frankly sexual way that sparked a thrill of arousal deep inside her. She couldn't help but notice the unyielding ridge behind the button fly of his jeans.

She smiled. "I think I found that hidden weapon."

Jamie chuckled throatily. "Shouldn't you check and make sure? You wouldn't want to be mistaken about a thing like that."

Her gaze was drawn inexorably to that severely strained button fly. Again he was inviting her to be the one to take things a step further. The problem was, even before the lightning, she'd been unused to having control in sexual situations. Now, after four years without human touch, she wasn't quite sure if she knew what to do.

She hesitated long enough that he said, "Darlin', if you're not comfortable with this—"

"Shh." India silenced him with a kiss, a long one, during which she brought one hand slowly around to the front of his jeans. She paused briefly, then pressed it over his erection, capturing his spontaneous moan in her mouth. She stroked him through the coarse fabric, gratified to feel his entire body tighten in response.

When she started undoing the buttons, he broke the kiss. "India . . . darlin'. I'm not going to lie to you. If we do this, it's going to get to the point where . . . I'm not going to be able to stop. Even if you want me to."

"I won't want you to." She reached under the waistband of his white Jockeys and closed her hand around his hot flesh.

He groaned. "Oh, God." After only a few seconds of her fondling, he seized her wrist. "If you do that, I won't be able to last. I don't want to disappoint you."

India studied Jamie—six and a half feet of nonstop male in unbuttoned jeans, golden and virile in the firelight—and laughed inwardly at the notion that he could ever, in a million years, disappoint her. If anyone blew it, it would be her. What if her mental TV switched on at an inopportune moment and she panicked?

He gathered her in his arms. "Nothing bad's going to happen." He'd read her mind. Was that his blue sense or just deductive reasoning? Or could it be that special affinity lovers were supposed to share? "It'll be beautiful," he murmured reassuringly, then placed a hand over the juncture of her thighs, lightly fondling her through the denim. "Let me show you."

She nodded. He unzipped her jeans and squatted down to slide them over her hips and fling them aside. Now eye-level with her gold satin string bikini panties, he grinned in appreciation. "Oh, those are very nice. I like those a lot." Then, taking her by her hands, he pulled her down onto the thick rug and laid her gently on her back.

She reached for him. He settled onto her carefully, conscious, probably, of his size. Their mouths met in a searing, endless kiss, their legs—hers bare, his still clad in jeans—tangling as they moved together in an instinctive rhythm. He rolled them to the side and cupped her satin-covered bottom, then slid a hand beneath her panties and around to the front, over her damp pubic hair. He paused as if waiting for her to stop him. When, instead, she covered his hand with her own and pressed it against her, he lowered it and slid a long finger deep inside. India gasped with pleasure.

"You're so wet," he murmured as he caressed her intimately. "I want so much to be inside you."

She was ready for him—more than ready. She tore at his jeans and Jockey shorts. He sat up with his back to her and swept both off quickly, then pulled a little packet out of his wallet and ripped it open. India wriggled out of her panties, relieved that she didn't have to bring up the subject of protection. Wrapping her arms around him from behind, she reached down and stroked him sensually.

"India . . . that feels too good. You'd better not. You'll make me lose control."

"I want you to. I want us both to." She did. He'd been holding back all along, pacing himself, treating her as if she were made out of spun glass. But she didn't need that, didn't want it. She wanted him to take her with primal abandon, as he had in her amazingly erotic dream. She wanted to join with him in a wild, unthinking frenzy. After four years of sensual famine, she was in the mood for a feast!

He made a sound like a groan crossed with a chuckle as she escalated her efforts to drive him to the edge. "Stop, darlin'. Please."

Something made her say, "Make me." Abruptly he turned, grabbed both her wrists, and pinned her to the rug with breathtaking speed. He wore a "this'll-teach-you" grin, but his eyes glittered with genuine hunger. His strength and the intensity of his need excited her enormously. He kissed her so hard, it almost hurt. Parting her legs with his knee, he released her hands and reached beneath her to lift her hips.

He had barely positioned himself to enter her when her mental TV switched on, and she cried out, struggling. All she saw was herself, in a blinding procession of images bursting one after another across her field of vision. All her thoughts were his and his alone, all her feelings those of a painfully aroused man about to bury himself deep inside a woman—inside her!

Jamie's voice joined the cacophony in her mind. "The remote, India! Picture the remote. You're holding a remote. Press the Off button."

The remote. The remote. With a tremendous effort of will, she managed to do as he commanded. She pressed the imaginary little red button and the mental bombardment ceased.

When she opened her eyes, she found herself lying on her back, Jamie hovering solicitously over her. "You all right?"

She nodded. He lay on his left side next to her, his back to the fire, and she curled into his embrace.

He kissed her hair, lightly massaged her back. "What triggered it? Do you know?"

"I think so," she mumbled into his woolly chest. "I think what happened was I just reached a . . . a threshold. I was able to block out your feelings until they got to a certain point. . . ."

"A flash point," he said. "Like when paper gets to 451 degrees and suddenly bursts into flame."

"Like that, yeah. I guess I can only take so much . . . well, heat."

"Things tend to get pretty hot when people make love, darlin'. We may have a bit of a problem here."

She groaned. "A problem? It's a tragedy. For me, at least. I really wanted this. I wanted so much to make love to you."

"Whoa." Jamie backed away a bit so he could look her in the eye. "I just said we had a problem. Problems can be solved. I'm not very good at admitting defeat, remember?"

"Yeah, but—"

"India, you say you want this. With me, it goes beyond wanting. It's right up there with breathing, at this point. I need you. More than I've ever needed any woman. I need to make love to you. And I'm going to. Tonight."

India found her defeatism evaporating under the weight of Jamie's single-minded determination. She actually smiled. "All right, hotshot. I'm waiting for the brilliant plan."

He settled down again and stroked her hair. "I've been thinking. Your fear of touch manifests itself in the form of other people's thoughts and feelings."

Smoothly put, India thought, reflecting that he'd just restated—albeit diplomatically—his conviction that her ESP wasn't for real. He considered it a psychological aberration, just as Perry and her parents had. The fact that she was lying naked in Jamie's arms right now made his disbelief all the more painful. She had never intended to let him get this close to her. A relationship with James Keegan could only bring her more of the anguish she'd spent four years trying to escape. *Don't think about it tonight*, she commanded herself. She'd have to deal with it soon, though, and she didn't relish the prospect.

"You've made some progress in keeping these episodes from occurring," he continued, "but the truth is, they may never go away entirely. Ten years from now, something may trigger one."

"Where's the brilliant part?" she asked dispiritedly.

"I'm coming to it." He rose up on an elbow, his right arm draped protectively around her. "The problem isn't really the episodes themselves, but the fact that you panic when they happen to you. You feel helpless, out of control. I'm thinking that maybe the key to dealing with episodes like this is knowing—*really* knowing—that you can turn them off at will." He frowned in thought for a moment and then asked, "Have you ever gone downhill skiing?"

"Sure."

"You know that out-of-control, panicky feeling, your first time out, when you're speeding down that slope and you're not sure you can stop?" She nodded. "But then you get good at stopping, and everything's great after that. Not only do you not panic anymore, you actually enjoy the experience."

"Are you saying I might someday enjoy my psychic episodes, as long as I know I can turn them off?"

"Sure," he said. "Why not? As long as you *really* know you can turn them off. With absolute certainty. So much so that even when you get ambushed by one, like you did just now, all you have to do is—" he shrugged "—push the Off button." He kissed her and enfolded her in his arms. "The next time it happens, don't panic. That's the important thing—don't panic. Stay calm. Take a deep breath. And then picture that remote in your hand."

"I'll try," she whispered.

"Good. Now, close your eyes."

"Why?"

"Irritating wench." He kissed her eyelids closed. "Because I said so."

"Yes, Lieutenant," she mumbled as he began drawing his fingers through her hair.

"And breathe in deeply, then let it out slowly. And again." He stroked her lightly as he urged her, in a low, soothing voice, to let go of her tension, to concentrate only on what she was feeling. India's response to the now familiar routine was so ingrained that she felt its tranquilizing effect almost instantly.

"Feel the rug underneath you," he said. "Feel my body next to you, and the heat from the fireplace. Feel my hand, touching you." He trailed his fingers over her face, her throat, her breasts and hips. "Feel me touching you. Just that. Just my hand on your skin." He traced paths of heat all over her body, heat that awakened as it soothed.

India felt him ease her onto her back, but he stayed close, his mesmerizing caress never pausing. She sensed warmth near her mouth, and then the whispery movement of his lips as he murmured, "Focus on where I'm touching you. Let everything else fade away."

He kissed her lightly, then glided his hand down her belly, and lower, to explore her damp heat. "Just feel this," he whispered as he worked his magic, coaxing her gradually into a state of breathless arousal. She heard soft moans and realized they were hers. She felt movement, and knew she was writhing with pleasure in his arms. In the midst of this sweet delirium, she became dimly aware of him shifting himself, and her, so that their legs were scissored together, he still on his side next to her, she on her back.

"Just feel," he whispered as another sensation joined that of his caressing fingers—the sensation of pressure as he prepared to enter her. "Just feel." She felt him push in, just a little, and then stop. "What do you feel?"

"Heat," she murmured, opening her eyes to meet his intent gaze. "Stretching."

"It's been a long time for you. It's not uncomfortable...?"

"No, it feels tight, but...wonderful."

"Yes." He pressed in slightly further. "Incredible."

She wondered how it felt for him, then quickly banished such speculation from her mind. *Just feel just feel just feel.*

He continued touching her as he filled her, little by little, speaking softly to her, taking his time. The effect was intoxicating; she'd never felt so inflamed, never been kept hovering so long on the brink of release.

Sweat-dampened hair hung across his forehead. She felt a shudder pass through him, and he closed his eyes, his body taut, his face flushed. *Just feel just feel just feel . . .*

But this time the TV did click on. She stilled, strange new sensations gripping her body as her mind exploded with fleeting images—her pale skin, her soft breasts, her ethereal eyes. *Don't panic. Don't panic.*

Taking a deep breath, she visualized the remote in her hand and knew she could stop this any time she wanted. That knowledge gave her the confidence to pause a moment and consider, as a matter of curiosity, exactly what it was she—or rather, he—was feeling.

She felt his tightly clenched muscles, the knot of pleasure in his groin, but most of all the enormous strain of holding back . . . for her. She felt a current of tenderness within him, felt his deep concern and affection for her. But most of all she felt the extraordinary thrill of hot, wet flesh closing tightly around him, inciting him to drive himself deep into her warmth—an urge he struggled to rein in, for her sake. *Hold back . . . take it easy . . .*

Enough. In her mind's eye she pressed the red button on the remote, and in a heartbeat she was herself again, looking into his eyes, glazed as if with fever. She guided his head toward her and kissed him. He wrapped his arms around her.

"You don't have to hold back, Jamie," she whispered.

"But—"

"Please don't." She reached down, pressing on his hips as she lifted hers.

Jamie groaned as he sank deep inside her.

"Please," she breathed as she flexed her hips again. "I want this."

That was all it took. Abandoning his resistance, Jamie thrust again, and again, deeply but at a wonderfully unhurried pace. India met his languid strokes, their sweat-slicked bodies writhing in intuitive rhythm. She felt drunk with pleasure, losing track of time as he kept her suspended, trembling on the edge of climax. He knew just how to move to drive her to the limit and hold her there, backing off now and then to make it last before renewing his efforts.

"Jamie," she panted, feeling her fingers dig into his hips. He, too, was shaking with his need; she knew he was close. "Oh, Jamie, please. Now."

He touched her lightly where their bodies were connected. It was like pushing a button. Pleasure exploded inside her and she cried out, shuddering violently.

"Yes," Jamie whispered hoarsely as he caressed her, extending her climax for so long that she thought she might die from gratification.

As her pleasure ebbed, he locked his arms around her and shifted, deepening his penetration. His entire body quivered, every muscle tight as he drove into her with increasing urgency. He moaned and threw his head back, his body rigid.

India's mental TV flickered on, but all she saw was blinding white light. She instantly squeezed her eyes closed, picturing the remote. *Don't panic.*

Her overriding sensation was of a white-hot, excruciating pleasure centered in her groin...*his* groin...no, *hers*. She thrust her hips reflexively, and a growl of fulfillment rumbled all around her as that pleasure spread in pulsing waves throughout her body. She heard her name called out, and her own shuddering groan as the pleasure erupted, pumping from her in hot, fierce bursts.

Two voices cried out in unison; two bodies quaked with a single, shattering release.

"INDIA? DARLIN', open your eyes. Please."

With a supreme effort, India lifted her heavy eyelids and saw Jamie's face, very close to hers, his eyes wide with concern. She felt softness all around her and saw that she lay on the sofa, naked under an afghan. He knelt beside her. "Jamie?"

He let out a giant lungful of air and cupped her face with his big hands. "Thank God. I thought maybe you'd stroked out or something. I was just about to call for an ambulance."

"What . . . what . . . ?"

"You fainted, I guess. A couple of minutes go." A lopsided grin replaced his worried expression. "Was I that good?"

She chuckled, but it emerged as a growl. "Oh, my God, Jamie. Oh, my God . . ."

He laughed incredulously. "Yeah, it was pretty amazing. Especially at the end. I thought you were done, and then . . . God, it was wonderful. What happened?"

"You wouldn't believe me if I told you."

He lay down next to her and gathered her in his arms. "Try me."

She bit her lip. "Remember when you said I might actually be able to enjoy my psychic episodes, as long as I knew I could stop them?"

"You mean . . ." He blinked. "You're saying that's what happened at the end? You felt me . . . you felt it when I . . ."

"Everything."

He nodded carefully.

"You don't think that's possible," she said. It wasn't a question.

He kissed her forehead. "It's awfully tempting to think it is. It would be incredible, if that could really happen." He took a deep breath. "But the truth doesn't care what we *want* it to be. It just is."

A great sadness engulfed India. "So you still don't believe me. Even a little bit."

He ran his hands through her hair. "Darlin', it's not a matter of belief, exactly. It's more a matter of interpretation."

India thought about that. She captured his gaze with hers and said quietly, "No, it's not, Jamie. I wish it was, but it's not. It's entirely a matter of belief. Of faith. Your faith in me. I'm sorry, Jamie, but I can't just shrug off your disbelief the way you want me to. Especially now, after . . . after tonight."

He studied her for a moment. He didn't look happy. "What are you saying?"

The phone rang before India could formulate an answer.

Jamie sighed irritably. "I'm on duty. I have to answer that in case it's for me."

He crossed the room and picked up the phone in the corner. "Keegan. Yeah, hi, Sam. What's up?"

In the dim light of the dying fire, India saw that he'd put his jeans back on while she'd been unconscious, but clearly rather hurriedly. They were only halfway buttoned, revealing a patch of dark hair where the white of his Jockey shorts would have been had he bothered with them. She closed her eyes and looked away, wishing he wasn't so damned sexy.

"Son of a bitch," Jamie growled. A pause. "Where was the body found?"

India sat up, wrapping the afghan around her.

Jamie looked at his wrist and grimaced to find it bare. "It's what, about nine-thirty? Do me a favor, Sam. Send a uniform over to keep an eye on—" He smiled briefly, but it never reached his eyes. "You *are* one step ahead of me. Thanks. Yeah, Len will do—just barely. I'll head on over there now. Tell those clowns not to even *think* about touching anything unless they're looking for a demotion."

He dropped the receiver in its cradle.

"Who's dead?" India asked, shivering now that the fire was little more than embers.

He grimly recrossed the room, buttoning his jeans. "Darrell Finn, of two gunshot wounds to the chest. A wino stumbled over him in an alley off Division Street about twenty minutes ago."

"Who—"

"Who do you think?" He grabbed his sweater with the T-shirt still inside it and yanked them down over his head.

"No," she said as he sat on the edge of the sofa to tug on his socks. "I don't believe it. Tommy wouldn't—"

"Tommy would." He attached his ankle holster, checked the little revolver and replaced it, then pulled on his sneakers and tied them. "I don't want to believe it, either. But that doesn't make it any less possible."

"Jamie, please. Hear me out."

"I don't have time to hear you out, India." He rose, swiftly buckled on his shoulder holster, and slipped the big blue steel pistol into it. A banging sounded at the front door. "That'll be Len. I've got to go." With a smile he nodded toward her bare shoulders peeking out from the afghan she clutched around herself. "Go on upstairs now before you give the kid a heart attack."

He kissed her quickly but thoroughly, then strode toward the door, saying, "We'll talk when I get back."

INDIA TREMBLED and wept as they strapped her down for the electroshock treatment. Indifferent doctors and nurses tightened the bindings and checked the equipment, muttering things she couldn't understand. She struggled frantically against the restraints, begged to be let go, but they ignored her completely.

Perry was there, offering cocktails to her parents.

But I'm not crazy! she screamed.

Of course you are, Perry replied silkily. *You're completely insane.*

He turned and handed a drink to Jamie, who accepted it with a bemused chuckle. *Silly girl thinks she can read minds.*

She awoke with a moan of despair, then covered her face with her hands and curled into a ball. "Oh, Jamie," she whispered hoarsely into her pillow.

JAMIE CAME BY at noon and sat in the waiting room until India was finished with her last appointment. She found him hunched over, elbows on knees, contemplating the object he held, wrapped in black plastic and tagged as evidence. When she sat on the chair next to him, he wrapped a hand around her head and drew her face to his for a lingering kiss.

Finally he released her, then looked back down at the plastic-wrapped bundle, turning it over thoughtfully. India expected him to say something about the case, but instead, he said, "Have you ever been to Ireland?"

"No."

"I haven't been there since I was ten, but I've been thinking about going back, just for a visit. Have you ever heard of Dunmore, on the south coast?"

"Is that where you grew up?"

He shook his head. "We lived nearby, in Waterford. My da cut glass in the factory, when he was working. Waterford's nothing special—just an ugly old port city. But Dunmore . . ." He smiled wistfully; his accent, India noted, was particularly strong this morning. "It's not much, just this little fishing village, but going there is like stepping back in time. It's an innocent place, a very simple place. And very beautiful. The countryside around there is all rolling hills, the greenest you've ever seen. And the ocean's like a living thing. The waves can hit the shore so hard, they shoot up the cliffs and down into the chimneys of the houses on top." He grinned at her skeptical expression. "You don't believe me. I should take you there and show you."

"No, I believe you."

He took her hand. "I'd like to take you, anyway. Not now, but in June or July, when it's warm. I remember this inn. Very quaint—thatched roof, the whole nine yards. You'd love it."

"I don't know . . ."

He gave her hand a squeeze. "Just you and me, India. And the rest of the world can go to the devil, just for two weeks. What do you say?"

"Jamie, I . . ." She shrugged helplessly.

"You don't have to answer now. Just think about it, all right?"

She nodded. Biting her lip, she lowered her gaze to his big hand, wrapped around hers. She was way too close to opening up her heart to him, way too close to saying, yes, take me to Ireland, take me away, make love to me forever and ever and ever. She could love this man, could give herself completely to him. But then what? How long could she sustain a relationship with him before the weight of his disbelief destroyed what they had?

She cleared her throat. "Have you eaten? I'll make you something."

He sighed and released her hand. "Don't have the time." He opened up the black plastic, revealing an olive green canvas knapsack, from which he withdrew a flat, nickel-plated pistol. "I've got to get this to forensics, but Sam wanted me to bring it by so you could—" he shrugged "—you know. Do your thing."

"A reading?" He nodded without looking at her. "Is that the murder weapon?"

"Most likely."

"Did you find it in the alley?"

"No, there was no weapon in the alley. Just Darrell— dead about six or eight hours by my guess, but the coroner will tell us for sure. I did, however, find two spent casings that came from a .32 caliber semiautomatic, like this one. A .32 auto is the only kind of gun I've ever known Darrell to carry, and his piece was missing. That led me to believe he'd been shot with his own gun, which was then removed from the crime scene by the killer."

He rubbed his jaw. "I wanted to find the gun, but I thought I should talk to Missy first, so I went to her place—this little apartment by the train station. She had a black eye, a fresh one—Darrell's handiwork. Turns out she's had a restraining order against him, but he didn't pay much attention to it. She turned white when I told her her husband was dead. First thing she asked was whether Tommy did it."

"Really?"

"Remember, at the lumberyard, when Tommy threatened to kill Darrell if he ever came near Missy or the baby again?"

"Yeah, but—but that was just talk."

"Talk leads to action, India. I got an arrest warrant drawn up and went to Lorillard. Tommy was at his locker in the basement, getting ready to leave. He put on a pretty good display of surprise when I told him his cousin was dead. Almost had me going for a minute there—till I found this—" he handed India the shiny little gun "—in his locker, hidden in the knapsack."

The weapon was smooth and cold and heavy in her hand. "Are you allowed to search someone's locker without a warrant?"

"I can search anything within arm's reach of the guy I'm arresting. That's how I found the magazines under Tommy's bed the other time." He sighed raggedly. "Tommy really lost it when I came up with the gun. Started screaming that he'd been framed. Screamed all the way to the station, screamed the whole time he was being booked. He actually came up with an alibi for the night of the lumberyard fire, but I don't buy it—he'd say anything at this point."

"What's his alibi?"

"He says he's been staying with Missy at night, to protect her from Darrell. I asked him why he didn't just tell us so in the first place, and he said he thought it would look bad for Missy to be cohabiting with a man while she's trying to fight for custody of her son."

"Sounds reasonable to me," India said.

He shrugged. "Alibis generally sound reasonable. It's not hard to come up with a good one if you put your head to it, or to get someone to corroborate it, the way Missy did this one. The judge wasn't that impressed. He set the maximum bail. It's so high, there's no chance of him ever coming up with the bread. He's in for keeps this time." He nodded toward the gun. "So, what do I tell Sam? Any psychometric vibes?"

India closed her eyes and held the gun between her palms. The lingering energy was muffled, as it often was with inanimate objects, but clearly recognizable. "There's a lot of Darrell here. You can tell Sam this was definitely his gun. There's a little bit of you, too, just from recent handling. No one else."

"No Tommy?"

She shook her head. "No, Tommy's never fired this gun."

"You don't know that for sure," Jamie said. "Maybe he wore heavy gloves while he did it."

"If we're talking about heavy gloves, it could have been anyone, couldn't it? It didn't have to be Tommy."

He dropped his head into his hands. "Yeah, but it was."

"How do you know?"

"I know. Look, I don't like this any better than you do—"

"Here." She returned the gun to him and took the knapsack, holding it in her lap with her eyes closed. She fingered the rough fabric, feeling the muted buzz of Tommy's psychic energy, and nothing else. "This belongs to Tommy," she said. "It was probably already in the locker when the killer went to hide the gun in there. It's full of his vibes, but they're all . . . I don't know how to describe it. They're benign. Harmless. There's no way he ever murdered anybody."

"India, please. The facts are the facts."

"Tommy's innocence is a fact, Jamie. I *know* it, and if you'd just listen to your blue sense instead of denying it so stubbornly, you'd know it, too. Tommy Finn did not kill his cousin."

"I need proof, India, not just wishful thinking."

"I have the proof right here in my hand."

"That knapsack? That's not proof."

"To me it is."

He shook his head slowly. "Then I guess we'll just have to disagree about that." He took the knapsack from her and replaced the gun inside, then secured it within the black plastic.

India thought her words out carefully. "Jamie, I don't think you understand, not really. This isn't just something else we can 'agree to disagree' about. This is too important. It has to do with what I am, who I am, intrinsically. And it has to do with your faith in me."

He set the evidence bag on the floor. "Look, I know you've had some bad experiences. I know you've been hurt—"

"I've been worse than hurt, Jamie. I've been through hell, twice. First with my parents, and then with Perry. All I ever wanted was just for the people who said they cared about me to have a little faith in me. And that's all I want from you—just a little faith."

"Darlin', asking me to believe in ESP is like asking me to believe that the world is flat." He laid a hand gently on her cheek; it struck her that he looked completely drained. "I have to get this to forensics, India. And then I'm going to get some sleep." He leaned over and kissed her. "I want to take you out to dinner tonight. A real date. How would that be?"

"I don't know, Jamie. I don't think so. I need some time to think."

There was a long pause while Jamie searched her eyes. Finally he got up and turned to stare out the window, hands on hips. "Don't do this, India," he said quietly.

"Do what? I just need some time—"

"Darlin', I'm thirty-four years old. I know damn well what it means when a woman says she needs some time to think. You're burning me off."

"Jamie...I'm sorry. It's my fault, for letting myself get involved with you. It really wasn't a good idea."

"Not a good idea?" He spun around, his expression incredulous. "I don't know about you, but I've been thinking last night was just about the best idea I've ever had. I've never—*never*—experienced anything like that. And now you're asking me to just shrug it off like it was nothing."

"You're asking *me* to shrug off your disbelief in me. I can't, Jamie. I *can't*. Don't you understand that?"

He came and knelt before her. "We can work it out. Let me take you to dinner tonight. Talk to me. Tell me what it's like for you when you have a psychic experience. Let me try to understand..."

"So you can analyze my delusion? Decide exactly what kind of nut I am, and then try to cure me?"

"India..."

She took his hands, her throat tightening, her eyes stinging. "Jamie, please. Don't make this harder than it has to be. You can't imagine how grateful I am for what you've done for me. You've enabled me to touch people again. But we've reached an impasse here, and I don't think there's any way through it."

"There isn't, if you won't give it a chance. I know you're scared—"

"I'm terrified. I'm—" She choked back a sob as tears slid down her cheeks. "I just don't think I can go through

it all again—that hell of trusting someone, loving someone, and having them think I'm c-crazy. It would kill
me." She broke down, crying in earnest.

"Shh . . ." He gathered her in his arms and patted her
back. "All right, darlin'. All right. Hush now. That's
right." He pulled a handkerchief out of his pocket and
dabbed at her face. "Tell you what. I'll give you what you
originally asked for—a little time to think. I'll back off
for a while. I don't have to stay here at night, 'cause
Tommy's behind bars—he's not a threat anymore."

Tommy was never the threat, India knew, but she kept
the thought to herself. Nine days had passed since the
Firefly delivered his note to her, and no attempt had been
made on her life. Most likely the whole thing really *had*
been a bluff, just as Jamie had thought. She'd lock her
doors at night and leave the lights on; no harm would
come to her.

Jamie kissed her eyelids. "How would that be? If I just
gave you some time? So you could relax and get used to
the idea of being with me?"

"Jamie, please don't expect that to happen," she replied brokenly. "I can't be with you if you don't believe
in me. No amount of time will get me used to the idea."

"Give us a chance, India," he said huskily.

He tilted her chin up and brought his mouth close to
hers, but she wrested her head to the side and rasped,
"Please go. Please."

He stilled, his body tight as a bow. Finally he picked
up the evidence bag, rose, and walked to the door. He
opened it and stood for a long moment with his back to
her, ignoring the chilly breeze that swirled in from outside. "I'll call you."

"Don't. Please."

His shoulders sagged. "Is this really want you want?"

She swallowed hard as fresh tears poured down her face. "It's what I need. I'm sorry, Jamie."

"So am I."

He shut the door behind him and walked away.

9

"THE ESPRESSO HERE is superb," Alden said. "But not if you let it grow cold."

India tore her gaze from the window next to their table, through which she'd been watching a young couple kissing on the sidewalk, her mind consumed with thoughts of Jamie. Four days had passed since she'd last seen him—four empty days, four days of loneliness and misery. She'd asked him not to call, and he hadn't, but that didn't stop her heart from racing with anticipation every time the phone rang. Afterward, she'd chastise herself for her weakness. Sometimes she'd cry.

She looked down at her tiny ceramic cup, still filled to overflowing with inky Italian coffee, a sliver of lemon peel untouched on the saucer next to it. "I'm afraid I haven't been very good company, Alden." She picked up the peel and twisted it, squeezing out fragrant beads of lemon oil, which she rubbed onto the rim of the cup.

Alden drained his cappuccino and dabbed his mouth with his napkin. "Oh, I don't mind a bit of silence. But it troubles me that you seem so out of sorts. Especially since I had ulterior motives for inviting you to breakfast. Makes me feel like a cad."

India smiled. "You're the only man I know who can get away with using the word *cad*—or with wearing an ascot, for that matter." She sipped her lukewarm, lemon-scented espresso as she studied Alden. The ascot was a deep burgundy paisley, very rich looking against his white silk shirt and brass-buttoned navy blazer. "So, what are your ulterior motives?"

"First tell me what's bothering you."

Her gaze returned to the window; the young couple was gone. "Several things."

"Could one of them be James Keegan?" He chuckled at her nonplussed expression as he withdrew a box of Dunhill cigarettes from his inside pocket and opened it. "Do you mind?"

"No, but this is the nonsmoking section."

"Is it? I didn't notice." He slid out a cigarette and tapped it on the table, clearly unconcerned. "It's perfectly obvious Keegan doesn't credit your powers. Curious—he seems a bright enough sort. One would think he'd be more open-minded."

"You're the only person who's ever believed in me unequivocally," she said.

He struck a match. "I pride myself on being quite unlike everyone else."

She grinned knowingly. "A cut above?"

He lit the cigarette. "How about 'a breed apart'? Sounds more egalitarian."

"Since when have you been egalitarian?"

He chuckled good-naturedly. "You're changing the subject. We were talking about you and your troubles."

"I'd rather talk about you and your ulterior motives. Care to share them with me?"

He drew thoughtfully on his cigarette. "It's about that young man they arrested."

"Tommy Finn?"

Alden nodded and sat forward, his elbows on the table. "You worked with Keegan on the case. Tell me the truth. Do you think Tommy murdered his cousin?"

India drank some espresso and replaced the little cup carefully on the saucer. "No."

"Do you think he set those fires?"

"No."

He sat back, his gaze never leaving hers. "Neither do I, but I wanted your opinion. I know that kid. He's worked for me for six months. I couldn't believe he was guilty, but I had to be sure."

Her eyebrows rose. "You put that much stock in my opinion?"

"Your gifts make your opinion worth more than most people's." He caught the waitress's eye. "Check?"

India raked a hand through her hair. "I feel so helpless, Alden. An innocent man is in jail, charged with arson and murder. I keep thinking there's something I should do."

"What could you possibly do?" He took the check, plucked some bills from his wallet, and fanned them neatly on the white tablecloth.

She shrugged. "Try to figure out who really committed those crimes?"

"Keep the change, Mary," he told the waitress as she scooped up the bills.

"Thank you, Mr. Lorillard."

As the waitress walked away, Alden said, "You can't be serious. Don't you think that's dangerous?"

"Do I have any choice?" she asked. "Everyone just assumes Tommy is guilty. But my powers give me access to information that's not available to everyone else. Maybe I should use them to try to identify the *real* Firefly. *And* the real murderer."

"Perhaps they're one and the same," Alden said, stubbing out his cigarette.

"Perhaps they are. Who's in a better position to find out than me?"

"Who indeed?" They rose. Alden took her shearling coat from the back of her chair and held it open for her. "Just promise me you'll be careful."

"I will."

THAT EVENING Jamie stood on the front porch of India's house, feeling absurdly nervous over the prospect of ringing her doorbell. Finally he took a deep breath, let it out, and pressed the little button. After what seemed like an eternity, the porch lights went on and the door opened.

Her eyes glowed like burnished gold coins when she saw who it was. "Jamie." A hint of something—happiness?—softened her features, but only briefly. She swiftly shuttered her expression, her hand unconsciously reaching up to close the collar of her oversize white shirt—the same shirt she had worn the night they'd made love.

He cleared his throat. "You should ask who it is before you open the door. I could have been anybody. I could have been Tommy Finn."

"Tommy Finn's in jail."

"Not anymore. He made bail late this morning."

She blinked. "But I thought you said he couldn't afford his bail."

"He couldn't. Alden Lorillard posted it for him." She just stared at him. "Can I come in?"

She stepped aside and he entered the foyer. "I should have known," she murmured. "I should have realized that's what he intended to do."

"What do you mean?"

"I had breakfast with Alden this morning. He wanted my opinion about Tommy—although it seemed to me he was half convinced of his innocence already. He just wanted me to confirm what he was already thinking." She raised her chin defiantly. "But I'm not ashamed for having confirmed it, and I'm glad he bailed Tommy out."

Jamie chose his words with care, not wanting to alienate her before he'd even had a chance to try and patch things up. "Darlin', I know you have your reasons for thinking Tommy's innocent. But I'm afraid you may have gotten your wires crossed somewhere along the line." He pulled the folded-up photocopy out of his coat pocket and handed it to India. "This came a couple of hours after he was released."

India unfolded the note and read it. She actually paled slightly, and for a moment Jamie regretted having shown it to her. She read the note out loud. "'This one will light up the night sky. They'll see it in outer space. You'll be telling your grandchildren about me.'" She looked up at Jamie, her expression guarded. "Where's Tommy now?"

"Gone. Disappeared from the face of the earth the moment we let him go, near as I could tell."

She closed her eyes for a moment, then took a deep breath, refolded the note, and handed it to him. "Did you come here just to see the expression on my face when you told me all this?"

"I came here to spend the night," he said, shrugging off his trench coat. Her eyes widened and then narrowed. "Purely in my capacity as a public servant. Tommy's on the loose again, and he may still feel you pose a threat to him. I'm here to protect and defend. Nothing more."

He hung his coat up in the front closet, then unbuttoned his suit jacket; he'd come here straight from work, not bothering to change into comfortable clothes.

She folded her arms across her chest. "Couldn't you have gotten Len or somebody to watch over me? Do you have to do this yourself?"

"Absolutely." He took her by her shoulders and implored her with his eyes to meet his gaze. "This is *my* job, my responsibility. I have to make sure you're kept safe." He kissed the top of her head. "It would kill me if anything happened to you."

She took a step back. "I was just about to go upstairs and watch TV for a while before I go to sleep. I'll see you in the morning, Jamie."

He slid his hands slowly down her arms, and then released her. "Good night."

AN HOUR LATER, Jamie knocked softly on her bedroom door, rehearsing in his mind the things he would say to her. *The past four days without you have been hellish for me, India. I've been so sure of myself, so wrapped up in my idea of what's possible and what's not. All I'm sure of now is that I need you—more than I've ever needed anyone or anything in my life. Talk to me. Tell me about your gifts. I'll try to believe, I swear to God. I'll listen with a totally open mind. Just talk to me.*

His knocks having gone unanswered, he quietly swung the door open and crossed the room, his gaze on the big, spindle-backed bed. India lay fast asleep against a pile of pillows atop the undisturbed white comforter, the remote control cradled in her hand. The TV was still on, although the sound was off; its cold light flickered over her, making her ivory skin even paler and giving a bluish cast to her white satin nightgown.

When he got closer, he saw that the nightgown's bodice had a triangle of translucent netting sewn into it, revealing the rounded inner swells of her breasts. At one edge of the insert he could just make out part of a dusky nipple. The urge to reach out and touch it was almost irresistible. He wanted to lie down next to her and pull her into his arms, lift her nightgown and bury himself deep inside her. His need was sudden and overwhelming—almost painful.

Better get out of here, Keegan. He unfolded the blanket at the foot of the bed and draped it over her, then leaned down and gently kissed her cheek. A soft murmur escaped her, and he saw her chest begin to rise and fall more rapidly.

Forget it, Keegan. Get out. Jamie carefully slid the remote out of her hand, turned off the TV, and went back downstairs.

INDIA AWOKE AND SAT UP in the dark, breathless and intensely aroused. "My God," she whispered, dragging her hands through her hair. "Was that a *dream?*" She replayed it in her mind—Jamie coming to her in her bed, lifting her gown, taking her with desperate abandon. She had absorbed his raging need; it had become her own need, her own overwhelming hunger.

Switching on the bedside lamp, she noticed the blanket over her and realized Jamie had been there. Had he touched her? Was that what had spawned that incredible dream? She held her hands out; they quivered. Her entire body seemed to vibrate with sexual energy. Her breasts ached; she could feel the heat and dampness between her legs.

There was half a bottle of Chablis in the fridge, left over from a chicken-in-wine dish she'd made for Jamie last week. A glass of that might be just what she needed to get her relaxed enough to go back to sleep. Tossing aside the blanket, she rose and threw on her kimono, then crept silently downstairs and into the darkened kitchen. She opened the refrigerator, blinking at the glaring light. The wine turned out to be hidden behind a barricade of milk containers and juice bottles on the top shelf, and it took her a minute to get it out.

She shut the door and turned, then gasped, nearly dropping the bottle. Jamie stood watching her from the kitchen doorway, lit from behind by the hall light. He'd shed his suit jacket. His tie was loosened, his shoulder holster very black against his white shirt.

She backed up against the refrigerator, unable to wrest her eyes from his as he walked toward her. Feeling suddenly short of breath, she held the bottle up as he came to stand over her. "Would you like some wine?"

"No," he said quietly, taking the bottle from her and setting it on the counter. He held her gaze for a moment, and she saw a raw desire in his eyes that was more than a match for her own. When he reached for the silken sash at her waist, she made no move to stop him from untying it, although she knew she should. The kimono slid open. She shivered with longing as his big hands closed over her swollen breasts, squeezing gently. The cold air from the refrigerator had chilled her; she felt his heat through her nightgown and moaned softly.

He glided a hand toward her lower belly. "Jamie . . ."

"Shh." He kissed her deeply as he caressed her through the liquid-smooth satin, his touch igniting her already sensitive flesh. He seized her hand and molded it to the front of his trousers, guiding it up the length of his erection. Her body betrayed her with a lightning flash of arousal. She needed him inside her. Now. Nothing else mattered.

He unzipped his fly and closed her fingers around his straining shaft, hard as polished marble. Raising her gown, he slipped a hand between her thighs, growling deep in his throat to find her already wet.

With swift, sure movements, he lifted her and wrapped her legs around him, supporting her under her hips. She grabbed fistfuls of his shirt and held on, groaning as he filled her, crushing her hard against the refrigerator with a single stabbing thrust. Already on the verge of climax, she bucked against him, moaning his name.

"Oh, India. Yes!" He withdrew his full length and drove in again, and a convulsive pleasure grabbed hold of her, shaking her senseless. His thrusts grew fierce and quick as the tremors rippled through her. The refrigerator rocked under the assault, creaking in time to his harsh breathing and her breathless cries. Soon she felt the hot surge of his own release within her, heard his low, ragged groan of completion.

His arms trembled as he held her, his breathing gradually becoming steady. India became aware of a sharp pain in her chest and realized his gun had dug into her. "Jamie," she said, looking down at the livid red indentations on her skin.

"Oh!" He bent down and kissed the angry marks. "You'll have bruises." He eased her down onto her feet and adjusted their clothing. Something seemed to occur to him as he zipped up his fly, and he grimaced. "I didn't wear a condom."

"I didn't think of it, either," she said, feeling weak-willed and remorseful. The situation had slipped out of her control again, and that shamed her. "I didn't think at all."

"Neither did I. I'm not sorry, though. I mean, I'm sorry that I didn't use protection, and that I hurt you—" he lightly touched the marks on her chest "—but I'm not sorry it happened." She studied the floor. "*You're* sorry," he said, his voice tight with emotion.

"I don't know how I feel. I'm confused."

"You weren't confused a couple of minutes ago. You knew just what you wanted. So did I."

"What I want and what's best for me aren't necessarily the same."

He cupped her cheek. "Aren't they?"

"No. This was a mistake. This shouldn't have happened."

"India . . ." He tilted her chin up, but she turned her head to the side before he could kiss her.

"Let me go, Jamie."

She turned to leave, but he grabbed her arm. "We need to talk."

She wrested out of his grip. "We *have* talked."

"India—!"

She left the kitchen and climbed the stairs. He called after her once, but didn't follow her.

THE PHONE WOKE INDIA UP. She groaned as she fumbled for the receiver, wondering why she bothered, since it was probably for Jamie. "Hello," she mumbled as she heard the downstairs extension being lifted; Jamie was listening in.

"India? It's Alden."

"Alden?" India sat up and looked at the digital clock on her night table. It was 3:27 a.m.

"I know, I know," he said with a rueful chuckle. "I feel awful bothering you in the middle of the night, but I've got a . . . rather unusual situation I'm dealing with here, and it seems you're the only one who can help."

"What's the problem?"

"Are you aware that I posted bail for Tommy Finn this morning?"

"Yes. That was quick work. It may be tacky to ask, but how'd you come up with the money so fast? I was led to understand . . . well . . ."

"That my business is failing?"

"I'm sorry, Alden. It's none of my—"

"Nonsense, my dear. You're like a daughter to me. The fact is, I had to call in a favor and borrow the money from a friend."

She raked her fingers through her hair. "Well, I hope you get it back. Are you aware that Tommy disappeared as soon as he was released?"

"Yes, and I know about the new arson note. Tommy didn't send it."

"Are you sure?"

"I've always prided myself on my ability to judge human nature, India. Tommy Finn is innocent." She heard him take a deep breath. "And he wants to prove it."

"What are you saying? Are you in contact with him?"

"He called me about an hour ago and asked me to meet him at my warehouse. That's where I am now—we're both here. He has some evidence that could exonerate him, but I told him he should let you give it a psychic reading first, to make sure it's what he thinks it is."

"What? I don't under—"

"It's difficult to explain over the phone. You'd have to see it. I'd like you to come down to the warehouse and take a look at it, if you wouldn't mind."

"Now?"

"I know it's asking a lot. But an innocent man's life is at stake."

India chewed on her bottom lip for a moment. She didn't relish the prospect of this clandestine meeting in the wee hours of the morning, especially considering the fact that she was no longer unequivocally convinced of Tommy's innocence. But if he *was* innocent, and she could help him . . . Alden would be there, she reminded herself. She wouldn't be alone with Tommy; the risk wasn't really so great. "Okay. I'll be there in half an hour."

"I knew I could count on you."

India stripped off her nightgown and was half-dressed by the time Jamie knocked on her door a minute later.

"Go away!" she called.

Without a moment's hesitation, he opened the door and walked in. He'd put his suit jacket and trench coat back on.

"Where are *you* going?" she asked.

Glancing at her black leggings and pink lace bra, he said, "I was about to ask you the same question."

"You listened in on the call." She sat on the edge of the bed and pulled on a sock. "You know where I'm going."

He stalked toward her. "Not if I have anything to say about it."

She slipped on the other sock. "Well, you don't."

"That's where you're wrong." Before she could register his actions, he whipped a pair of handcuffs out from under his trench coat and grabbed her right hand.

"What are you doing?" she shrieked as he snapped a cuff around her wrist.

"I should think that'd be fairly obvious." He brought her hand toward the bed's headboard and fastened the other cuff to one of the wooden spindles.

She yanked at the cuff; the heavy stainless steel dug into her wrist. "Damn you, Jamie! Unlock this thing! Let me go!"

"It's for your own good, darlin'. Not to mention being a most flattering accessory for that particular outfit." He trailed his fingertips down her throat and over a lace-covered breast. "You wouldn't believe how sexy you look right now."

"I hate you!" She balled her left hand into a fist and swung it toward his face.

He seized her wrist before the blow could connect, and smiled. "I'm sorry to hear that, 'cause I'm head over heels in love with you."

She stared at him, thunderstruck.

"You didn't realize I was falling in love with you?"

"I—I don't know."

"You don't have to say it back," he said. "You just have to let me do this." Taking her face between his hands, he kissed her with fierce passion.

He released her, and she drew in an unsteady breath as he walked away. "Jamie, please unlock these cuffs before you leave."

Pausing in the doorway, he gave her a quick once-over and grinned devilishly. "Darlin', I may not even unlock them when I get back!"

For about ten minutes after Jamie left, India worked on trying to slip her hand through the cuff, reasoning that she was a good deal smaller-boned than the average felon, and might have a shot. All she got for her troubles, however, was a badly abraded hand.

She looked around for anything within reach that might be of help, and her gaze lit on the stacks of wooden cases on the mantel—specifically the flat, brass-trimmed one that housed the Cossack dagger. Could she successfully pick the lock on the handcuffs with it? Probably not. Did she have to try? Absolutely. Alden and Tommy would be there at the Lorillard Press warehouse, waiting for her, only to have Jamie show up instead. What would he do when he found Tommy? Take him back into custody, most likely. They'd trusted her, and she felt as if she'd unwittingly betrayed them by letting Jamie eavesdrop on that call. She had to free herself and get to the warehouse as soon as possible.

Her right hand was shackled to a spindle fairly close to the edge of the headboard. Standing, she was able, by stretching her left arm as far as it would go, to just barely touch a corner of the mantel; the case she wanted was unreachable by about a foot. With an exasperated whimper, she threw herself at the mantel, only to howl in pain as the cuff bit into her already raw flesh.

The wrought iron stand that held the fireplace tools was also out of reach, but by extending her leg, she found she could hook a stockinged foot around it and tug it toward her. It toppled forward, the tools clattering onto the slate hearth. The poker landed nearest to her; she caught the hooked tip with her toe and dragged it close enough to grab.

Carefully she reached out with the poker, hooked the case containing the dagger, and pulled it toward her, which caused the cases in front of it to fall off the mantel like dominoes. She winced as one of them flew open, sending a pair of dueling pistols tumbling out. Dropping the poker, she took the flat case, sat on the edge of the bed, and opened it.

She lifted the sheathed dagger and immediately flinched and dropped it. Flames filled her vision, leaping up all around her, searing her flesh.

Gasping, she stared at the weapon on the floor by her feet. It looked as it always had, with its carved horn hilt and velvet scabbard ornately mounted with steel. Leaning down, she gingerly touched it again, reminding herself that the flames weren't real; they couldn't hurt her.

She saw them again, leaping and dancing all around her. She felt their heat—and something else. A presence, a human presence, but one devoid of human warmth. She sensed a profoundly arrogant man, one who felt himself to be the center of all things—a higher life-form unfettered by the rules that applied to everyone else.

Aside from Jamie, the only person who had touched this dagger within the last few months was Alden. He told her he'd used it to open letters.

Summoning all her mental strength—*the flames aren't real, the flames aren't real*—she picked up the dagger and unsheathed it, wrapping her hand around the slender, gold-inlaid blade as she closed her eyes.

The flames subsided, and now she shivered as the icily arrogant presence settled around her. Her ears were filled with a sinister humming, like a thousand wasps droning inside a nest. The sound took form, coalescing into words, as if someone were hissing into her ear...

My matchbook is whispering to me.

"Alden?" she murmured in bewilderment.

She heard his quiet laughter... private laughter, as if at some wonderful joke only he deserved to enjoy.

Something burns this week. And the next... and the next...

No. It was impossible. This was just some stress-induced delusion, not a true psychic reading. Alden wasn't the Firefly. He couldn't be. What possible reason would he have for burning down buildings in Mansfield?

An image took shape in her mind's eye—an old brick building. It was night, and she could barely make it out, but she knew with absolute certainty that it was the Lorillard Press warehouse. Even before the darkened windows erupted in flame, even before the fire swept through the building, consuming it in a hellish inferno, she knew that this was the final, devastating blaze that all the others had merely been leading up to. This was the one that would light up the night sky, the one they'd see in outer space.

The last fire. The one that would solve all his problems, the one that would free him of the financial albatross of Lorillard Press and enable him to retire in style . . . as long as he didn't get caught. Any loose ends would have to be eliminated. Any incriminating evidence could be consumed in the final fire . . . as could any potential witnesses, anyone who might be able to point the finger at him. Just get them to the warehouse, tie them up . . .

"Oh, God," India moaned. Alden had tried to lure her to the warehouse tonight. Her powers made her a threat to him, and he meant to . . . to eliminate her. To let her burn up in the warehouse. Tonight.

But Jamie had gone in her place.

"Jamie," she whispered. He was in danger, terrible danger. Alden meant to incinerate the warehouse tonight, she was sure—and any "loose ends" along with it.

The phone was out of reach on the other side of the bed. Taking up the poker again, she found she could barely touch it to the handset cord, dangling off the side of the night table. With a grunt, she stretched forward just enough to snag the cord with the hook. "Gotcha!" She pulled, and the receiver tumbled out of its cradle and fell onto the bed.

She furiously punched out 911, drawing a shaky breath as a female voice asked her what her emergency was.

"There's a . . . a police officer who's in trouble. Please. You've got to help him. Send someone—"

"Are you with this police officer now, ma'am?"

"No. No, I'm—"

"Then how do you know he's in trouble?"

"I'm a psychic," India blurted out. From the ensuing silence, she gathered this revelation had been a serious error. "Please. You've got to believe me."

"Ma'am . . ."

"Please. I know it sounds crazy, but—"

"This number exists for genuine emergencies, ma'am."

"This is not a crank call!" India insisted. "Please!"

"If a police officer needed assistance, he'd radio the department," the woman scolded. "Please don't use this number in the future, except in the case of an emergency."

Click.

India aimed the receiver to throw it, then thought better of it and dialed information for Sam Garrett's number.

"That number is unlisted," announced a voice that sounded eerily like the 911 woman.

"Bitch," India snapped.

"What?"

"Sorry," she mumbled, and hurled the receiver across the room. As she stared at it, lying in the corner, the idea came to her that she could call the police department directly. She grabbed the poker again, but was unable to retrieve the phone from where she'd thrown it. "Brilliant," she muttered. "Just brilliant."

She yanked ineffectually at the handcuff for a while, then took the dagger and jammed its tip into the little keyhole, knowing even as she did it how futile it was to try to use such a crude instrument for such a delicate job.

"Please..." she moaned as she frantically wriggled the blade in the lock. "Oh, please . . ."

10

JAMIE STOOD in the darkened parking lot of Lorillard Press and knocked on the door of the windowless brick warehouse. "Alden?" He knocked again. No answer. Turning the knob, he found the door unlocked. He opened it slowly; the interior was pitch-black and eerily silent. It had that smell old buildings acquire over the years, that faint, deeply ingrained mustiness. A wave of apprehension crawled over him.

Something's wrong.

He felt on the wall until he found a light switch, which he flipped, igniting dozens of bulbs dangling by wires from the exposed beams that crisscrossed the high ceiling. The warehouse was all one cavernous room filled with row after row of tall steel bookcases stacked with shrink-wrapped volumes and cardboard boxes. "Alden?" Still no answer.

Yes, something definitely felt wrong here. Maybe he should listen to his mental warnings and call for backup.

He shook his head. *Yeah, right.* Mental warnings . . . as in blue sense? There *was* no such thing. Nothing was wrong; he was just keyed up. Nevertheless, he unbuttoned his trench coat and jacket to give him better access to his gun, should he need it.

He stepped inside, stopping in his tracks at a sound from somewhere at the rear of the huge room. Holding his breath, he listened for a few more seconds. There it was again, a faint shuffling sound. Drawing his weapon, he silently negotiated his way through the maze of steel shelving, flattening his back to it when he reached the end of a long row perpendicular to the back wall. Whatever was making that noise was right around the corner.

Jamie took a deep breath and let it out. *Now.*

He swung around the corner, aiming low at the dark form on the wooden floor. A person. Tommy Finn.

Bound and gagged.

"What the hell . . ."

Tommy struggled against the ropes lashing him to the shelving, straining to talk despite the swath of electrical tape over his mouth. He emitted muffled sounds of distress, his eyes wild.

"Easy," Jamie said. Reholstering his gun, he squatted down and reached for the tape, but the young man shook his head frantically. "Take it easy."

Tommy's eyes, wide with alarm, shifted to look over Jamie's shoulder.

Keegan, you idiot! Jamie reached for his gun, knowing even before the blow came from behind, filling his skull with blinding pain, that he'd blown it. Bad.

His last thought as he slipped into unconsciousness, facedown on the floor, was that India had been right all along. He should always listen to his blue sense.

INDIA SCREAMED in frustration as she hurled the useless dagger across the room. With a helpless sob, she yanked again on the handcuff, hard, this time drawing blood. Grabbing the spindle it was shackled to, she pulled on it, but it didn't budge. She hammered the headboard with her fists, then collapsed against it, tears stinging her eyes.

No. No crying. Think. Think!

Opening her eyes, she examined the headboard, studying the way the spindles were set into the wood at the top and bottom. If only she had a crowbar. . . .

Grabbing the poker and holding it steady with both hands, she jammed its pointed, curved tip into the little gap between the bottom of the spindle she was handcuffed to and the bedframe. She twisted, and heard a faint creak. She twisted again; the gap widened, and she forced the tip in farther. For long minutes she worked this way, prying away at the loosening juncture, until at long last she heard the blessed crack of splitting wood.

SENSATION CREPT BACK into James Keegan's consciousness in the form of a smell—the distinctive, all-too-familiar smell of kerosene.

He opened his eyes and found himself lying on his side on the floor of the warehouse, staring at two large metal cans set against the back wall, about ten feet away—most likely the source of the odor. One of them had a smear of blood on the bottom edge. From somewhere in the labyrinth of shelves he heard splashing, accompanied by whistling—The *1812* overture. He tried to rise, which made the back of his head pulse with pain, and called his attention to the fact that he was tied up.

Congratulations, Keegan. You really aced it this time.

He took a moment to assess his situation. His hands were bound behind him. When he tried to move them, he found that they'd been secured to the corner strut of the bookcase in back of him. His ankles were tied together, too, but apparently his ankle holster hadn't been detected; he could sense the weight of his snub-nosed Colt .38 against his leg. His shoulder holster felt empty, though.

With considerable effort, he hauled himself into a sitting position, leaning against the strut. The back of his head throbbed, and he felt warm rivulets of blood trickling from the open wound there. He closed his eyes for a moment, willing the pain to fade, then turned and looked around the corner. Tommy was still there, bound and gagged. "Hi," he said lamely.

Tommy nodded.

Jamie indicated the bloodstained kerosene can with a tilt of his head. "Is that what I got coldcocked with?"

Tommy nodded again.

Jamie wriggled his hands, testing the ropes that held him; they were very tight. He inspected the shelving. Each strut was bolted securely to the wooden floor.

He turned toward Tommy again. "Doesn't look good, does it?"

Tommy shook his head.

Jamie said, "Guess I had it all wrong about you, huh?"

Tommy rolled his eyes.

"Sorry, man. India told me. She knew. She . . . she senses things." He shook his head. "I had my reasons for not believing her," he murmured, more to himself than to Tommy. "I guess they weren't very good ones."

Tommy gave him a thoughtful look and nodded.

"Oh, I'm *so* glad you two have patched things up." Jamie turned to see Alden Lorillard setting down an empty kerosene can. "A pity it's going to be such a brief friendship." He wore a tweed sport coat over a tan cashmere turtleneck, and Jamie was struck by the idiotic thought that this was what the well-dressed businessman wore to burn down his warehouse.

And the people inside it.

Alden opened the sport coat and withdrew Jamie's 9 mm Sig-Sauer from the waistband of his pleated charcoal trousers. "A most impressive weapon, Lieutenant. I should get one of these for target shooting." A wave of shame engulfed Jamie. Not once in his entire career had he let his weapon fall into the hands of a perpetrator—until now.

The perpetrator in question racked the slide on the big blue steel auto, squatted down, and placed the barrel firmly against Jamie's temple. "I've never been very patient with uninvited guests, so I suggest you answer my questions quickly and with a minimum of prevarication. Should you do otherwise, I think you'd find the consequences most distressing. Can I speak plainly?"

"I doubt it."

Alden smiled slowly, his thin lips pressing together into something that looked like a really bad paper cut. Transferring the gun to his other hand, he whipped the steel grip across Jamie's forehead with surprising strength.

Blinding pain detonated behind his eyes. His vision filled with bursts of light, and his senses whirled drunkenly. He felt his hair being grabbed and his head being yanked up. Opening his eyes, he found Alden's face about six inches from his.

"Where's India?" Alden demanded grimly.

Jamie forced a smile. "Just a stone's throw from Sri Lanka. You can't miss it."

Alden raised the pistol and brought it down on Jamie's head with savage force. His head exploded with red-hot pain. A second blow caught him in the nose; he heard the crunch of cartilage, and his head lolled forward. He felt the gun barrel beneath his chin, lifting it up and digging into his throat.

Jamie opened his eyes to find that one was swollen almost shut. Grimacing, Alden jammed the barrel hard into his windpipe. "Where the hell is she?"

"Piss off," Jamie rasped, bracing himself for a few more cracks with the pistol grip.

Instead, Alden studied him at length, his expression transforming from furious to knowing. "She's at the house, isn't she? How did you keep her from coming here?"

I handcuffed her to her bed. She'll be completely at your mercy when you walk in and aim my gun at her. Jamie swallowed hard, his expression carefully neutral; he tasted blood. "She doesn't know anything about your involvement in the fires, Alden. She's no threat to you."

That humorless smile sliced across Alden's face again. Rising, he tucked the Sig-Sauer back into his trousers. "I don't leave loose ends, Lieutenant. I'll have to take care of her as soon as I'm done here. Should be a simple matter to make it look like young Tommy's handiwork."

Stall him, Jamie ordered himself as Alden unscrewed a fresh can of kerosene and began pouring it onto the floor between the rows of shelving. *Don't let him get to India!* "I take it this is an insurance scam." He flexed his hands in a desperate attempt to loosen the ropes.

Alden smirked. "Brilliant deduction, Lieutenant."

"And the other fires were a setup. So that when your own business got torched, the insurance company would think it was just the Firefly's latest escapade, and pay up."

"Oh, you *are* bright," Alden drawled as he spilled the kerosene in neat, intersecting paths. "You would have made a splendid replacement for Captain Garrett, if only you could have lived that long."

"Did you kill Darrell Finn?"

"You're the one with all the clever answers. What do *you* think?"

"I think you did. Mind telling me why?"

From behind some shelving, Alden said, "This is beginning to sound rather tiresomely like an interrogation, Lieutenant. I don't think you quite appreciate your position here."

"It can hardly have escaped me. I just thought you might be gentleman enough to satisfy my curiosity before you light the match." Jamie thought he saw a flash of movement in the stacks off to his right. Or was that just his overstressed mind playing tricks on him? "Did Darrell find out that you set those fires? Is that why you killed him?"

"Ah. So you're not so clever, after all." Alden chuckled. "It was Darrell who set those fires—for twenty thousand dollars. Or rather, the promise of twenty thousand dollars. As it turns out, all he cost me was the price of two bullets. Does that answer your question?"

Out of the corner of his eye, Jamie saw it again—a flutter of movement, something—someone—ducking behind the row of shelves to which he was bound. There was the glimmer of metal—handcuffs dangling from a wrist.

India! She got free! He closed his eyes for a moment— *No. Please, India... Get out! Now!*—then forced his gaze back to Alden. *Keep him talking. Act normal.* Normal? What was *normal* about this situation? "Did you send the notes, or did Darrell?"

"Are you kidding? Every member of that family is functionally illiterate. I could never have trusted Darrell with that side of things." Clearly warming to the subject, Alden shook the last of the kerosene out of that can and traded it for a full one. "Which is not to say he didn't possess a certain measure of native cleverness. It was his idea to point the finger at Tommy by planting misleading evidence—his wallet and those magazines. Of course, his motivation was rather petty. I gather he was jealous over Tommy's interest in that trampy little wife of his."

Jamie heard thumping and turned to see Tommy thrashing against his bonds, his eyes glittering with fury. "Easy," Jamie murmured.

Alden snickered at Tommy's impotent outburst. "So reassuring to know that chivalry's alive and well in Mansfield . . . although perhaps not for long." He continued methodically dousing the floor.

Jamie felt cool fingers wrap around his, and he sucked in his breath. India was right behind him, reaching between the cartons on the bottom shelf to touch him. He wanted to scream at her, to order her away. *Don't you see what this madman is planning? This place will go up like a bomb when he lights that kerosene. Get out of here! Forget about me!*

India couldn't see Jamie's hands, but she could feel them, through the gap between the cartons that shielded her from Alden's view. His fingers tightened around hers as his desperate pleas bombarded her mind.

"*Forget* about you?" she whispered. With her free hand she withdrew the Cossack dagger from the pocket of her sweatshirt and started sawing at the heavy rope knotted around Jamie's hands. "That's not an option. I'm going to cut you loose."

You can't. He'll see you . . . oh, my God . . . this is happening, isn't it? You're reading my thoughts. He wasn't that surprised, India sensed. He'd known it was possible. He'd already accepted it in his mind!

"Yes," she whispered. "But be careful. Don't let Alden suspect anything. Just look straight ahead."

For God's sake, India, don't do this! Leave now, while you can. Get out of here!

"No!"

Why not? he shot back.

"Because I love you."

There was no reply for a moment. She sensed amazement, joy, gratitude . . . and fear. He desperately feared for her life, even more than he feared for his own.

India . . . if you love me, get out of here. If I'm going to die, I want to die knowing you're safe.

"You're not going to die." The dagger at last cut through the rope. India breathed a sigh of relief and untangled it from his wrists. "Do you still have your guns?"

Just the snubby in my ankle holster. But I can't get to it with my ankles tied like this.

"Here." She closed his fingers around the handle of the dagger. "I'll create a diversion."

India—!

His objections were silenced when she removed her hand from his, breaking their psychic link. On silent, sneakered feet, she made her way back up the row of shelving, then peeked around the corner. Alden, having emptied the last can, set it down beside the others. By craning her neck a bit, she could see Jamie clearly for the first time since she'd entered the warehouse. She sucked in her breath at the sight of his battered, bloodied face. *Oh, Jamie . . .*

Catching her eye for a fraction of a second, he shook his head almost imperceptibly; he wanted her to leave. *No*, she mouthed. Alden turned his back to her for a moment as he reached beneath his sport coat, and India seized the opportunity to dart across to the stacks in back of him. She kept her eye on him as she stealthily crept down the row of shelves that separated them. The pungent smell of kerosene filled her nostrils.

Alden withdrew a pack of Dunhill cigarettes and placed one between his lips, then tucked it away and patted his pockets. "I do hope I haven't forgotten my matches."

India saw Jamie stiffen, but he did nothing to give away the fact that his hands were unbound. "Let us go, Alden. Leaving us here when you torch this place would be cold-blooded murder."

Alden produced the matchbook and grinned, as if it were all a marvelous joke. India froze, her heart pounding wildly at the prospect of being trapped in this building when it went up. Fire was her worst nightmare, her most primal fear, and the urge to flee to safety was almost irresistible.

Alden struck the match and lit the cigarette, then chuckled and blew it out. India exhaled shakily and kept going. That cigarette was as dangerous as the match—either one would ignite the kerosene on contact—but even if he meant to use it for that purpose, they might have a couple of minutes before he did so.

"Shooting Darrell Finn was fairly cold-blooded," Alden said, "but I assure you I haven't lost a moment's sleep over it. I'm afraid I don't share your rather sentimental objections to murder. Given a good enough reason, it's perfectly justifiable."

"No reason is good enough." India knew why Jamie was engaging Alden in conversation this way; he was trying to keep Alden from turning around and seeing her. She passed directly behind him, then kept moving in a direction parallel to the back wall, wanting to get as far away from Jamie as she could before she started making noise.

Alden expelled a stream of blue smoke. "Keeping you and India and Tommy from identifying me seems like an excellent reason. And in the case of Tommy, I might even end up getting my bail money back, once they manage to identify his remains. I suppose they'll have to use dental records—for both of you."

"How's it going to look, two bodies found in the ashes? How are you going to explain that?"

"I won't have to explain anything, because I won't be blamed for the fire. Tommy will, and he'll be dead. It will no doubt be assumed that he set it and then couldn't get out in time. As for your remains—" he shrugged and tapped the ash from his cigarette onto the floor "—perhaps you tried to stop him and, likewise, got trapped when the fire started. It's really of no concern to me how it eventually gets explained away. I'll be far away from here by then, sipping champagne on a beautiful white beach beneath fluttering palms."

India estimated her distance from Alden at about fifty feet, and decided that was far enough. Reaching up, she pushed a few heavy books off the shelf in front of her and heard them tumble onto the floor. There was a moment of silence, and then Alden murmured, "Well, well, well . . ."

India moved farther up the aisle, watching his image flicker in and out of view behind the stock on the shelves as he approached the scattered books. He held his gun— Jamie's gun—in one hand, the cigarette in the other. Right now, India considered both extremely lethal weapons. "It appears we have company. If I had to guess, I'd say the lovely India has decided to join us. What a delightful surprise."

India pushed a small box onto the floor. It landed with a thud and crashed open; Alden turned toward the sound, the gun outstretched. She continued making her silent way up the aisle, praying that Jamie was using this time to get free.

"Delightful for me, that is," Alden said as he slowly walked toward her, peering into the stacks. She held perfectly still, watching him through the gaps between the shrink-wrapped books on the shelves. "Your presence here provides a certain entertainment factor I hadn't counted on." He stopped, close to where she stood; she could see part of his face. Evidently he couldn't see her, but he had to know she was right on the other side of the shelves. He took a slow drag on the cigarette. "What do you suppose would happen if I tossed this over to your side? Let's find out, shall we?"

She looked down at the kerosene-drenched floor beneath her feet. Grabbing a steel strut in each hand, she braced a foot on a shelf and hauled herself up, just as Alden's cigarette soared gracefully overhead. Turning, she saw it land right in the middle of the kerosene trail. There was a heartbeat's pause, and then flame blossomed and spread in either direction.

India felt a wall of heat at her back, and heard Jamie scream her name. *Don't panic!* Swiftly she climbed to the top of the shelving, only to find Alden standing directly beneath her, aiming the gun at her head. She ducked as he fired, and the shot went over her head.

"Drop it! Now!" That was Jamie's voice! She looked up and saw him striding toward Alden, his snub-nosed revolver aimed at the older man. Behind him, Tommy was using the dagger on the rope around his legs. Good. He'd be able to get out on his own.

Wheeling toward Jamie, Alden squeezed off four quick shots. Jamie grunted and went down.

"Jamie!" India screamed as she scrambled along the top shelf toward where he'd fallen. Crackling rivers of fire coursed through the warehouse, and smoke began to rise toward the ceiling, but she forced herself not to think about what might happen if she couldn't get out. Jamie groaned and struggled to rise. *Get to Jamie... help Jamie.*

From the corner of her eye she saw Alden pivot toward her, the big pistol gripped firmly in both outstretched hands. Again she dropped, flattening herself to the steel shelf, but this time he anticipated that move and lowered the gun to keep her in sight. "Goodbye, India," he said calmly.

India flinched at the dull crack that rang out. It took her a second to realize she hadn't been shot. Alden sank to his knees, looking vaguely surprised. He started to raise a hand to the gunshot wound on his head, and then his eyes rolled up and he toppled sideways to the floor. He lay perfectly still, blood trickling from his mouth. India knew that he was dead. "Goodbye, Alden," she whispered.

Jamie, who had levered himself off the floor just enough to make the shot, met India's gaze for a fleeting moment, and then groaned and collapsed onto his back. His trench coat and suit jacket gapped open, revealing a dark stain on his white shirt, another on his left thigh. "No," India whispered hoarsely.

Turning, she climbed halfway down, then jumped the rest of the way when she found the contents of the lower shelves on fire. "Jamie!" She ran to his side and took him in her arms. Immediately she saw a flickering black-and-white image of herself, her eyes wide with concern...her incredible eyes...the most beautiful eyes he'd ever seen. She felt his relief that she was safe...his pain... his certainty that he was dying.

He touched her cheek, and then his hand fell to his bloodied chest. "Go," he whispered hoarsely.

"No way." He'd taken those bullets trying to protect her; she'd be damned if she was going to leave him now. She moved behind him, hooked her hands under his shoulders, and pulled, grunting with the effort. He was heavy, a couple of hundred pounds of deadweight.

"Please, India!" He coughed. So did India. The warehouse was filling with dark, acrid smoke. She felt the heat of the fire that swept through the kerosene-soaked stacks, leaving only the perimeter of the enormous room untouched. "There's no time. You can still make it if you go around the side."

She pulled again, dragging him mere inches. He was right; there was no way she could get him out of there before the warehouse was consumed. "Get up!" she yelled. "Walk! You can do it!"

He shook his head, his eyes half closed; he was losing consciousness. "Can't walk," he mumbled. "Love you. Go."

She shook him. "Jamie." She shook him harder. "Jamie!" Her eyes burning with tears, she screamed his name louder. "Jamie, please! Please open your eyes! Please get up! Please!" No response. She pressed two fingers to his throat and felt a weak pulse; he was still alive.

A hand on her shoulder made her shriek.

"It's me—Tommy."

Tommy. She could barely see him through the haze of smoke. He hadn't left, although he'd had the chance. He'd stayed to help. "Tommy!" she rasped, her throat constricting from the smoke. "Can you—?"

"Move aside." Coughing hoarsely, Tommy grabbed Jamie under his arms and lifted. "You take his legs."

Between them, they managed to pick the big man up and carry him. "This way," India directed, choking on the words. The smoke all but blinded her, and every halting breath burned her lungs. "Hurry! Keep low, and stay against the wall."

Even with Tommy's help, Jamie's limp form was a burden, making their progress around the edge of the large room excruciatingly slow. The fire raged like hell itself, roaring in her ears and blasting her with its heat. Sweat coursed from her in rivulets, and her whole body quivered with the strain of carrying on. She gagged and choked, thinking, *We'll never get out of here. We're going to die here. We're going to burn to death.* The alternative—dropping Jamie and making a run for it—was unthinkable. She loved him. She couldn't leave him.

"The door!" Tommy gasped.

India reached out a hand and felt blindly. It *was* the door! *Thank God!* She fumbled for the doorknob and twisted.

The door flew open. She and Tommy crumpled to the ground, gulping lungfuls of air as smoke billowed out of the warehouse, darkening the dawn sky. Dragging Jamie, they crawled across the parking lot until they couldn't crawl anymore, and then they collapsed onto the cold pavement, chests heaving.

Tommy sat up first. He was covered with soot and sweat, as was Jamie, and India herself. When he spoke, his voice emerged as a breathless croak. "I'll go find a phone . . . call 911." He struggled to his feet.

"Tommy . . ."

"Yeah?"

"You—you didn't have to do this. Thanks."

He shrugged. "Can't be a badass *all* the time." He stumbled off, hacking raggedly.

India laid Jamie out carefully on his back and took his pulse again; it was faint, but it was there. She tore at the bullet hole in his trousers to examine the wound to his thigh, finding a clean entrance and a jagged exit. The bleeding could have been worse.

She tried to unbutton his shirt, but her fingers trembled so badly that she finally just grabbed it and yanked it open, sending buttons flying. The wound was on the right side of his chest. It was small and neat, and appeared to have stopped bleeding—externally, at any rate. She knew that a wound like this could cause massive, life-threatening internal bleeding and damage to important organs; she hoped the ambulance came soon.

She lifted his head and cradled it in her lap, watching with a sense of unreality as the warehouse burned, its dark, reeking smoke staining a spectacular orange-gold sunrise. Using the hem of her sweatshirt, she wiped some of the soot off the uninjured parts of Jamie's face. His nose and one eyelid were badly swollen, and he was deathly pale. He moaned and mumbled something she couldn't make out.

"What's that, Jamie?"

He opened his eyes, amazingly blue against his soot-darkened skin. "I said I dreamed you were tearing my clothes off."

She chuckled. "I was."

He tried to laugh, but it deteriorated into a coughing fit. "Can't get enough of me, eh?"

"No." She leaned down and kissed him softly on the lips.

He smiled. "Then I guess you won't have any objection to marrying me—assuming I pull through."

After a moment's stunned hesitation, she said, as convincingly as she could, "Of course you'll pull through."

He coughed weakly. "Exasperating wench. Will you marry me or not?"

She took his face gingerly between her hands. "Yes." She kissed him again. "Yes." And again. "Yes. I'll marry you. Happy?"

"Very happy." He smiled, his eyes unfocused. "Deliriously happy." His eyelids lowered.

"Jamie?" She shook him. "Jamie?"

He murmured something.

"Jamie? What was that?" Closing her eyes, she concentrated, and heard the words in her mind as clearly as if he had said them out loud. *I love you, darlin'.*

From several blocks away came the shrill wail of sirens. "I love you, too," she whispered, holding Jamie tight and rocking him in her arms. "I love you, too."

Epilogue

THE OLD RED BICYCLE squeaked rhythmically as India pedaled it through the streets of Dunmore, reveling in the warm June breezes, fragrant with salt and seaweed. Jamie had been right, she mused as she wound her way through the bustling Irish fishing village and along the circuitous lane that led to the inn she had called home for the past week. He'd said that coming here would be like stepping back in time. That's why he'd wanted to bring her here—so they could escape together to a simpler, more innocent time, if only for two weeks.

She rode for some distance through emerald green pastures, enjoying the scenery and letting her mind wander. *I'll make a pot of tea,* she thought, smiling in anticipation. The room came equipped with an electric kettle and all the makings—although she'd used the last of the tea that morning, and would have to get some more. At last she rounded the final curve in the road and saw the inn at the end, its thatched roof gilded by the low afternoon sun. She parked her bike in front and went in.

"Mr. Leary?" she called from the lobby.

The innkeeper appeared in the entrance to the pub, a darkly paneled room off the lobby in which there were always three or four locals sharing a pint and a smoke. "Good afternoon, Dr. Keegan. And what might you be needin'?"

"Some tea, if it's not any trouble."

His wife came down the stairs bearing a stack of clean towels. "Captain Keegan asked me for tea not ten minutes ago. Said he wanted to have a pot ready when you came in."

"Really? He must have read my mind."

Mrs. Leary smiled knowingly. "Husbands and wives get that way after a bit, dearie."

Mr. Leary snorted. "They've only just got married, Fiona. They're on their honeymoon."

She scowled at him. "It doesn't take years if they're really soul mates, Paddy."

Her husband grunted and returned to the pub as India squeezed past Mrs. Leary and sprinted up the stairs. She opened the bedroom door and shut it behind her, blinking. In the middle of the small room, on a linen-draped table, sat a pot of tea, a creamer, a platter of sandwiches, a bowl of strawberries and a glazed cake. Looming over the table, his head nearly brushing the low, beamed ceiling, stood her husband, setting out cups and plates.

"Wow," she said. "That's some spread. Is that supposed to be a *snack?*"

His admiring glance swept over her body, clad in a cropped T-shirt and bike shorts. "You've got to keep your strength up."

She stepped into his arms. "My strength? What for?"

"For this." He closed his mouth over hers and kissed her deeply, his hands roaming possessively over her body. "And this." Scooping her up easily, he laid her on the high brass bed with its plush feather mattress and eased down onto her, thrusting his hips so she could feel the hard swell beneath his jeans.

She said, "I'm surprised *you've* got any strength left for this, after the past week."

Chuckling, he reached under her T-shirt to deftly flick open her bra and cup a breast. He lightly fingered her nipple, igniting a hot little spark of desire within her. "I'd have to be dead not to have the strength to make love to you."

He *had* almost died, she reflected as she studied his face, the face she had grown to love with such all-consuming passion: the midnight eyes, the boyish grin, the Roman nose now saved from perfection by an interesting bump about halfway down—a souvenir courtesy of Alden Lorillard. The internal bleeding from his chest wound had nearly cost him his life, after all. When they'd finally let her in to see him after the surgery and transfusions, he told her the only thing that had kept him hanging on was the fact that he'd get to marry her if he lived. Thinking about how close he'd come to dying made her shiver.

"Cold?" He lay next to her and gathered her in his arms. "But it's such a warm day."

"Mmm . . ." She moved sinuously against him. "I wouldn't mind if it got a little warmer."

"You read my mind."

"There's a lot of that going around." She kissed him until they were both breathless. "I want to make you crazy," she murmured against his lips. "Tell me what you want—what you really want."

He grinned. "You're the mind reader. You tell me."

She closed her eyes, pictured the remote, and pressed the On button. A silvery black-and-white image came into focus—an image from Jamie's perspective of her looking down on him, her legs astride him, as he lay on his back. She saw herself unbuttoning his shirt, felt his hunger for her.

"Mmm . . ." She rolled him onto his back and straddled him. Swiftly undoing his shirt buttons, she ran her fingers through the soft fur of his chest. The bullet wound had healed into a puckered little scar. Leaning down, she kissed it lightly, then took a flat nipple between her lips and gave it a gentle bite, making him moan.

"What else?" she whispered, closing her eyes. She saw herself from his view again, in glimmery soft focus, nude from the waist up—her high, round breasts, her delicate shoulders, her wonderfully narrow waist . . .

India whipped off her T-shirt and bra and tossed them aside. Jamie closed his hands over her breasts and arched upward, a low, feral growl rising from his throat. She mentally switched off the remote and reached for his belt buckle.

Some time later, as they lay naked and entwined and deliciously sated, India murmured, "Our tea must be cold."

Jamie pulled her closer. "I didn't really want it."

She stretched, little quivers coursing through her, and felt his body stir with renewed arousal. "Why'd you make it?"

He kissed her forehead. "You wanted it."

She molded herself to him, feeling a sweet, liquid heat pulsing through her. "How'd you know that, anyway?"

"My blue sense, I guess."

She chuckled. "Good answer, Captain."

He caressed her lightly. "Why don't you turn on that little remote control of yours and tell me what I'm thinking right now."

She smiled and kissed him. "I don't need ESP to know what you're thinking. You want to make love again."

Rolling on top of her, he lifted her hips and slid deep inside her. "And again, and again and again," he murmured as they rocked together in a dreamy, languid rhythm. "Until the end of time."

She smiled. "That's about how long I had in mind."

BRIDE'S BAY RESORT

UNLOCK THE DOOR TO GREAT ROMANCE AT BRIDE'S BAY RESORT

Join Harlequin's new across-the-lines series, set in an exclusive hotel on an island off the coast of South Carolina.

Seven of your favorite authors will bring you exciting stories about fascinating heroes and heroines discovering love at Bride's Bay Resort.

Look for these fabulous stories coming to a store near you beginning in January 1996.

Harlequin American Romance #613 in January
Matchmaking Baby by Cathy Gillen Thacker

Harlequin Presents #1794 in February
Indiscretions by Robyn Donald

Harlequin Intrigue #362 in March
Love and Lies by Dawn Stewardson

Harlequin Romance #3404 in April
Make Believe Engagement by Day Leclaire

Harlequin Temptation #588 in May
Stranger in the Night by Roseanne Williams

Harlequin Superromance #695 in June
Married to a Stranger by Connie Bennett

Harlequin Historicals #324 in July
Dulcie's Gift by Ruth Langan

Visit Bride's Bay Resort each month wherever Harlequin books are sold.

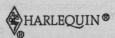

HARLEQUIN ®

BBAYG

Take 4 bestselling love stories FREE

Plus get a FREE surprise gift!

Special Limited-time Offer

Mail to Harlequin Reader Service®

3010 Walden Avenue
P.O. Box 1867
Buffalo, N.Y. 14269-1867

YES! Please send me 4 free Harlequin Temptation® novels and my free surprise gift. Then send me 4 brand-new novels every month, which I will receive before they appear in bookstores. Bill me at the low price of $2.66 each plus 25¢ delivery and applicable sales tax, if any.* That's the complete price and a savings of over 10% off the cover prices—quite a bargain! I understand that accepting the books and gift places me under no obligation ever to buy any books. I can always return a shipment and cancel at any time. Even if I never buy another book from Harlequin, the 4 free books and the surprise gift are mine to keep forever.

142 BPA AW6V

Name _____ (PLEASE PRINT)

Address _____ Apt. No. _____

City _____ State _____ Zip _____

This offer is limited to one order per household and not valid to present Harlequin Temptation® subscribers. *Terms and prices are subject to change without notice. Sales tax applicable in N.Y.

UTEMP-995   ©1990 Harlequin Enterprises Limited

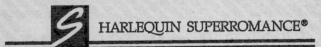

HARLEQUIN SUPERROMANCE®

From the bestselling author of
THE TAGGARTS OF TEXAS!
comes

Cupid, Colorado...

This is ranch country, cowboy country—a land of high mountains and swift, cold rivers, of deer, elk and bear. The land is important here—family and neighbors are, too. 'Course, you have the chance to really get to know your neighbors in Cupid. Take the Camerons, for instance. The first Cameron came to Cupid more than a hundred years ago, and Camerons have owned and worked the Straight Arrow Ranch—the largest spread in these parts—ever since.

For kids and kisses, tears and laughter, wild horses and wilder men—come to the Straight Arrow Ranch, near Cupid, Colorado. Come meet the Camerons.

THE CAMERONS OF COLORADO
by Ruth Jean Dale

Kids, Critters and Cupid (Superromance#678)
available in February 1996

The Cupid Conspiracy (Temptation #579)
available in March 1996

The Cupid Chronicles (Superromance #687)
available in April 1996

HARLEQUIN®

Temptation

Dreamscape

JASMINE CRESSWELL

Bestselling author Jasmine Cresswell makes her Temptation debut in February 1996 with #574 MIDNIGHT FANTASY. Heroine Ariel Hutton secretly longed for adventure and excitement in her life. Getting kidnapped by sexy, mysterious Mac was a start! Except Mac was *not* quite what he appeared to be....

Upcoming books by Jasmine Cresswell:

—*Weddings by DeWilde* series
SHATTERED VOWS (April 1996)
I DO, AGAIN (March 1997)

—MIRA books
NO SIN TOO GREAT (May 1996)
CHARADES (June 1996)
Look for these titles at your local bookstore!

JC

You're About to Become a Privileged Woman

Reap the rewards of fabulous free gifts and benefits with proofs-of-purchase from Harlequin and Silhouette books

Pages & Privileges™

It's our way of thanking you for buying our books at your favorite retail stores.

PROOF OF PURCHASE
HT-PP99
Pages & Privileges
Offer expires October 31, 1996

**Harlequin and Silhouette—
the most privileged readers in the world!**

For more information about Harlequin and Silhouette's PAGES & PRIVILEGES program call the Pages & Privileges Benefits Desk: 1-503-794-2499

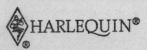

HARLEQUIN®

HT-PP99